"You're it," yelled Imogene, the self-appointed referee.

So, good-naturedly, Gabby sprang off the table and charged after Gus and Lassie. Gus took off across the barn floor, and Lassie jumped back up onto the table. Then she disappeared around a corner.

Sarah chuckled. Honestly, Lassie was acting practically like another kid, a kid with lots of fur. From the hayloft, Sarah was just about to call down something about Lassie being a fur kid when a loud crack shot through the barn.

Something slammed into Sarah, knocking her down. She sprawled on the loft floor. A sharp pain stabbed her left shoulder.

For a frozen second, silence loomed in the barn. Lassie barked her deep warning. . . .

Lassie™

HAYLOFT HIDEOUT

These heartwarming stories of a boy and his beloved dog Lassie have demonstrated the values of faithfulness, loyalty, and love to boys and girls for nearly five decades. As Jimmy and Lassie face different situations through the Lassie stories from Chariot Family Publishing, these same principles will come alive for children of the '90s in a way that they can understand and apply to their lives.

Look for these Lassie books from Chariot
at your local Christian bookstore.

Under the Big Top
Treasure at Eagle Mountain
To the Rescue
Hayloft Hideout
Danger at Echo Cliffs

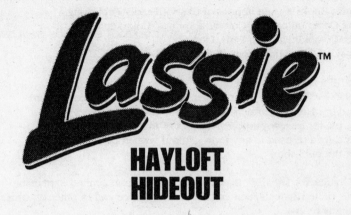

Lassie™

HAYLOFT HIDEOUT

Adapted by
Marian Bray

Chariot Books™
A Division of Cook Communications

Chariot Books™ is an imprint of Chariot Family Publishing
Cook Communications, Colorado Springs, Colorado 80918
Cook Communications, Paris, Ontario
Kingsway Communications, Eastbourne, England

Cover illustration by Ron Mazellan
Cover design by Joe Ragont Studios

First Printing, 1996
Printed in United States of America
00 99 98 97 96   5 4 3 2 1

Library of Congress Cataloging-in-Publication Data

Bray, Marian Flandrick
        Lassie, hayloft hideout / adapted by Marian Bray.
            p.   cm.
        "A Christian adaptation of characters and situations based on the Lassie television series"–
Front matter.
        Summary: When ten-year-old Sarah discovers a family of five children living in an abandoned
barn, she and her brother's dog, Lassie, come to their rescue.
        ISBN 0-7814-0265-4
        1. Dogs–Juvenile Fiction. [1. Dogs–Fiction. 2. Brothers and sisters–Fiction. 3. Christian life–
Fiction.] I. Title.
PZ10.3.B746Lap   1996
[Fic]–dc20
                                                                                    95-48794
                                                                                         CIP
                                                                                         AC

Table of Contents

Shattering the Peace

*B*rrrrrrrng. When the final school bell sounded, Sarah Harmon, 10, grabbed her backpack and headed for the door. She planned to run all the way home to avoid walking with her friends Monique Garcia and Brooke Cohn. Sarah was getting tired of the same old routine after school. She needed a change.

But mostly she just felt like running. She had spent the last fifteen minutes reading, and although she liked to read, she had picked a boring book this week. She needed to stretch her muscles.

Sarah was on dog duty today. Her brother, Jimmy, had asked her to walk Lassie, the family's tricolored rough-coat collie, when she got home. Jimmy had a special meeting after school and wouldn't be home until late. Sarah didn't mind. In fact, she looked forward to times when she and Lassie could do things together.

Lassie was the only one home when Sarah arrived. The collie greeted Sarah with her normal welcome-home bark and face lick. Lassie always made Sarah feel good—it was as though she had waited all day just for this moment. Sarah gave her a big hug. Lassie was as much a part of the family as Jimmy, Mom, or Dad. And even though Lassie was Jimmy's dog, today Sarah would pretend that Lassie was all hers.

"Want to take a walk, girl?" Sarah asked. The collie barked and wagged her long, silky tail. Sarah didn't need to snap a leash on Lassie; she never ran off. Jimmy called Lassie "a fur person," because she was so smart.

They walked along the road behind their house. The Harmons lived on the outskirts of the small town of Farley, Iowa. Sarah figured Farley was about as uninteresting as a city could get. Funny, that's how she felt about herself, too, . . . uninteresting and unimportant.

"Everybody is doing something important except me," Sarah told Lassie as they passed the last housing tract before the land rolled into crops and pastures.

Lassie whined at Sarah's sad tone. But Sarah only sighed. Even Lassie did important stuff. For example, Lassie had found a lost girl last Christmas Eve. She'd done other heroic things too. Sarah felt dumb, envying a dog, but Lassie always seemed to know the right thing to do. Sarah wished she knew the right thing to do.

"Take Monique and Brooke, for instance," she said. "They are planning this fancy party for Monique's eleventh

12

birthday. It's gonna be practically formal with fancy dresses. They're inviting boys, too! Ick."

Lassie barked as if to agree that Monique and Brooke were behaving outrageously. Sarah took comfort in the fact that she had one supporter.

"Then there's our family," Sarah said after a tractor trailer rumbled down the road. She counted family members on her fingers. "Dad's working overtime with the elders about starting a Christian elementary school at church." Dad was the pastor of their church, and he always did important things that honored God. Sarah couldn't think of much she did that God would be interested in.

"Mom," Sarah continued, "is on the board of directors for the Mary House, a place for unwed mothers. And Jimmy is the eighth-grade captain of ticket sales for the Wacky Rodeo. So what am I? A big nothing."

Lassie whined again and nudged Sarah's leg as if to say, I think you're wonderful.

So great, Sarah thought. *My dog thinks I'm terrific.* But Lassie's affection perked her up a little. She gave Lassie a quick hug, and then they cut through a field planted with red clover. A flock of sheep grazed peacefully nearby.

Lassie whined and stared at the bunch of sheep milling about in what seemed to be great tangled knots. Their odd yellow eyes watched her carefully. Then they moved quietly into one solid group.

"See?" complained Sarah. "You know how to herd sheep even though no one has trained you." She sighed noisily. Lassie nudged Sarah's hand with her damp nose, as if to say, It's different with dogs.

Sarah held down the lower strand of a barbed-wire fence so that Lassie could jump through. Then she carefully climbed through herself. "But I still feel like I don't do anything special. Not *can't*, but *don't*."

Sarah and Lassie crossed a two-lane road and climbed through another fence, heading for the pond. Sarah liked to walk around the lapping water and skip rocks over the tranquil surface. Maybe there she'd gain some peace of mind.

The most recent shattering event in her life was the election of the Wacky Rodeo staff representatives for KidsTown. Each grade competed against one another to sell the most tickets, and each grade had its own staff. Sarah didn't care about the rodeo itself; she wanted to become part of the ticket selling group. She didn't want to be captain like her brother, Jimmy, but she figured she could at least be one of the officers! She didn't get elected. She didn't even get nominated! Sarah still couldn't get over that.

Her supposed friend Brooke was elected secretary. And her other supposed friend Monique was assistant to the captain. And then, worst of all, Luke Castillo was elected captain of the fifth graders! Totally unfair. Sarah had had a massive crush on Luke forever. Then when she didn't even get elected to a small job with the ticket sellers, well, that was the crowning blow. Now Luke would be spending lots of time with Monique and Brooke, and she wouldn't be there.

"Of course, Jimmy just happens to be the captain of his class," she told Lassie as they climbed a low rise.

At Jimmy's name Lassie glanced around. "No, he's not here," said Sarah. "He's probably off selling a billion more tickets. And I've sold exactly four."

She tried not to remember that she had knocked on doors for less than an hour last week. But still. Only four?! What was the point if she could sell hardly any?

Sarah jumped over a small, neglected irrigation ditch thick with green, slimy water. One foot slid back and into the mucky stuff. "No fair!" Sarah screamed. She furiously clawed up the bank and snatched off her shoe. "I've almost ruined my new tennis shoes too!"

Lassie sprang neatly, landing in the rye grass on the other side.

Tears stung Sarah's eyes, but she wouldn't cry. She was too mad. Grimly she wiped her slimed shoe on the grass. She couldn't do much about her soaked sock, so she pulled off both socks, wadded them up, and threw them into the irrigation ditch. Then she put her shoes back on without socks. So there!

She stood up. The afternoon breeze trickled through

the abandoned field, lifting her long hair. The pond was just to the right. As she started that way, Lassie paused, head high, sniffing. She whined anxiously.

"What girl?" asked Sarah, searching the horizon. The pond was shrouded by weeping willows. The rise rolled down to an old farmyard a quarter mile away.

A tendril of gray smoke wavered up from the sagging barn. The small farm had been for sale for as long as Sarah remembered. Dad had said the soil of the old farm was poor, rocky, and in the past not cared for. The thirty acres would take a lot of work to get into shape.

The three-story farmhouse had been condemned, all its windows boarded up, and the doors nailed shut. The barn wasn't in much better shape. A good wind could easily flatten the building. It sagged at one end like a listing ship.

Nesting birds flitted in and out of the fallen boards. At night a curtain of insect eating bats soared into the night. When Sarah was younger, she and her friends used to tell each other that the barn was haunted. But the scariest thing about the barn was that at any moment it could fall down.

So was that really smoke or was she seeing things? Why was Lassie acting restless? The big collie whined, and without Sarah, trotted forward. Sarah hurried down the hill away from the pond after her.

Wacky Ticket Sellers

After school Jimmy Harmon, 13, stayed for a meeting with his Wacky Rodeo workers. His last class was algebra in Mrs. Brickley's room, so the four workers had agreed to meet there. They were helping to plan all the details for the mock rodeo that would take place in about ten days.

"I still think we should go for the donkey basketball," said Blake Smith, Jimmy's best friend. Blake was from one of the few African-American families in Farley, but that never seemed to bother Blake. Like Jimmy, Blake loved animals and had a great sense of humor. Jimmy thought Blake was cool.

The four eighth graders got up from the desks, the meeting over for the moment.

"Don't even start in about those donkeys," warned Katie Madison, the only girl on the team. "Or I'll whack you."

Jimmy stood back as his two friends faced each other, practically bristling. Jimmy and Katie had been friends a long time. He often helped her stock the shelves in her grandmother's hardware store. And even though she was a girl, she was no hundred-pound weakling.

Cal Freedman, the fourth member of the eighth-grade Wacky Rodeo ticket team, elbowed Jimmy with a grin. "Can't you civilize that girl? . . . You being the captain and all." Everybody knew that Jimmy and Katie were special friends—not just captain and teammate.

"Civilize me?" exclaimed Katie. She slammed her books back on the desk and her voice rose. "Civilize me? Did you forget I'm the one who has been going by Roberts rules of order for these meetings?"

"Robert who?" asked Cal.

"That's the last name of the guy who wrote a book about the official way to conduct a meeting," Katie said.

"It seems strange to me to be so strict about a meeting to plan a Wacky Rodeo," Cal said with a grin.

"Yeah, Katie, loosen up," Blake chided.

"How did this Wacky Rodeo get started, anyway?" Cal asked. "I never heard of it until we moved to Farley."

"About five years ago," Jimmy began, "KidsTown—that's the nineties' version of a home for foster kids and orphans—really needed money. They were going to have to close down. Dad and some of the elders in our church met and came up with the idea of having a wacky rodeo—kind of the Iowan version of a western rodeo. The city council loved the idea and has taken it on ever since."

"It brings in people from all over the state," Katie added, "and that means the visitors spend money here. That's good for our city, and we raise money to help KidsTown."

"And it gets all of us kids involved in a little friendly competition selling the tickets," Blake said.

"They also want the middle school kids to help plan the events," Katie smirked. "That's when it gets uncivilized."

"I guess they figured we'd come up with the wackiest events," Jimmy said.

"Okay, forget I mentioned donkey basketball," Blake said waving his hands in front of his face. "I have a better idea. We'll have two whacking teams, guys against girls."

Jimmy pretended to think it over. "Hmm, a whacking team in the Wacky Rodeo. Might just do the trick. So what will Blair Coughlin do?"

Blair Coughlin, the great quarterback from the Colorado Cobras, was coming to the Wacky Rodeo and Jimmy wanted to meet him.

"Not come to the rodeo," said Katie, "if he has an ounce of sense."

"Hey, he was the NFL's player of the year last season," said Blake. "He's got loads of sense."

"Dollars, too," added Cal.

They all groaned.

"For that bad pun, I'm assigning extra homework

tomorrow," said Mrs. Brickley over her shoulder as she closed the blinds.

"No fair," protested Jimmy.

"Then you'd better get out of my class as fast as you can," she said, a small grin itching to pop onto her face.

The four bolted into the hallway. "Gotta go to your locker anyone?" Jimmy asked generally.

"No, Mom," said Blake sarcastically.

Jimmy took a swipe at his friend, but Blake dodged easily. He was a head taller than Jimmy, and quicker than Jimmy with the moves. *But I'm faster in the long run,* Jimmy thought with a grin. He had trained for cross county even though his grade didn't compete. Next year he'd be in ninth grade and be able to run with the team.

As they walked off school grounds, Katie glanced at Cal in a way that Jimmy knew all too well.

"So Cal," she said. "What made you agree to be part of the ticket team?"

Jimmy knew that she meant, "Why does a guy who never says boo to anyone want to be on the ticket selling team?" Jimmy figured that Cal knew that Katie was suspicious of his motives too. The guy wasn't stupid or dense.

Usually Jimmy, Blake, Katie, and Katie's girlfriend, Jenny, did stuff together, such as work on committees or school projects. But when Jenny came down with a major measles attack (courtesy of her little brother), their homeroom teacher, Mrs. Brickley, had appointed Cal to the committee. Cal could have protested. He didn't.

Katie is almost being rude, Jimmy thought, but he wasn't sure how to stop her. Maybe she was mad because she was the only girl on the committee.

Cal shrugged his bony shoulders. He was not quite as tall as Jimmy, skinnier, not in a lean, fit way, but more like his bones stuck out at angles because there wasn't enough meat to go around.

Jimmy wondered why the usually silent, practically-a-wallflower—if you could call a guy that—Cal Freedman, had suddenly decided to be involved. Ever since Cal had moved to Farley last fall, he'd been one of those faceless kids, coasting through school, never drawing attention to himself, and never volunteering for anything. Now he seemed to like the idea of being on the committee. *Hey, can't a person change without it being a federal offense?* Jimmy thought.

"Lay off, Katie," Jimmy said very quietly. But Cal stiffened. Jimmy regretted saying anything. He meant it for Katie, not Cal. But Katie tossed her dark red hair and went in for the kill.

Boy, she gets huffy these days, Jimmy thought and rolled his eyes.

"Lay off what, James?" she asked, too sweetly, her clear voice ringing like a glass bell. "I'm merely asking Cal why he agreed to help with the tickets. That's all."

Jimmy just rolled his eyes again and dropped back to walk beside Blake on the sidewalk. Let Cal defend himself.

Blake silently shook his head at Jimmy, drew a finger across his throat, and pointed at Katie.

No kidding, thought Jimmy. Being captain could be a pain. Selling tickets was nothing compared to dealing with the others in his group.

At the moment he reminded himself that anything was worth the chance to meet number 42, Blair Coughlin.

Scared of Dogs

Smoke rose skyward in streams of gossamer gray. As the wind caught the stream, it was as if the smoke were steam puffs from a dragon's nostrils.

Sarah laughed at herself. Dragon, indeed! Actually she'd always felt sorry for the bad rap dragons got. Some storybook dragons were friendly, such as Puff the Magic Dragon, the dragons of Blueland, and Pete's dragon. When she was a kid—eight years old or so—she pretended she had a pet dragon. A small, fine-boned one, no bigger than a cocker spaniel, with long, soft, silky fur like Lassie's, only sea foam green. Her dragon had lacy wings and traveled everywhere with her, a beloved friend.

Sarah patted Lassie's head. "I guess I'd rather have a real-life friend like you, Lassie. But sometimes I wish I really did have a pet dragon. Having one would make me different, you know?"

Changing the subject, Lassie barked and broke into a trot toward the barn.

Was the fire worse? Sarah ran after the collie. *Where is the closest phone to call the fire department?* she wondered, and swiftly glanced around. Was the Murrey's farm the closest? They were at least a quarter of a mile back down the two-lane road. Should she run back to the road and wave someone down? No, Mom would have a fit if she found out Sarah was talking to strangers in cars. That would be practically as bad as hitchhiking, Mom would think.

Lassie reached the back of the old barn first. The smoke seemed to be in the front of the barn. Lassie darted around the side of the barn, with Sarah trailing after her. Lassie wasn't barking as if something were really wrong, so maybe it was a small fire, just started. Perhaps she could throw dirt over it.

As Sarah reached the back of the barn, she slowed, uncertain, her brain clanging warnings. A fire meant someone had started it. Maybe she shouldn't let anyone see her. What if it were some crazy, weird person? She almost laughed at herself . . . except crazies like that *were* around. She had seen news reports on TV.

Lassie still didn't bark. That was a good sign. Apparently, Lassie didn't think danger was near. Perhaps the fire started from faulty wires . . . but wouldn't the electricity be turned off?

Still cautious, Sarah crept around the two-story barn, staying within the afternoon shadows.

"It's okay, Lassie's friendly," she whispered. The girl from school stood over them, her hands on her hips, her eyes as big as the child's, but filled with what? Surprise? Fear? Sarah wasn't sure, except she knew the girl wasn't happy to see either Sarah or Lassie.

"If she's friendly," said the older girl, "why did she chase Imogene?"

Sarah suddenly recalled her name, a funny name—Briny. That was it. Their teacher Mr. Jackson, often said, "Earth to Briny, earth to Briny, are you there?" He sometimes said it in not a nice way.

But that was all Sarah knew about her. Except that she really didn't hang out with anyone. She kept to herself during recess and lunch and walked home alone. Sarah had noticed her, like someone sees the background, but never thought about it.

Lassie gently licked the younger girl's ear.

The two little kids, one a small boy, practically a toddler, had the same fiery hair as Briny. The girl under Lassie's paw had the same small pug nose as Briny, but her hair was the color of pure gold—the color Sarah would have done almost anything to have.

The little boy asked, "Is that dog going to eat my sister?"

"No!" exclaimed Sarah. She pulled Lassie back and said, "What are you doing, Lassie?"

"Are you okay, Imogene?" asked Briny, reaching for the

25

The red paint on the barn's massive sides had faded, and in places boards were missing leaving gaps in the wall. Because it was darker inside the barn than outside, she couldn't see in. However, someone in the barn would be able to see her. Sarah shivered.

Tall weeds rose around the far corner. A capped well was nearby. Sarah turned the corner of the barn, pushing past healthy bushes of yellow mustard flowers to the front face.

A child screamed and began to run. Lassie shot after the child, still not barking. They raced past a small, fierce fire burning in an old metal bucket. Sarah opened her mouth to call Lassie, when a girl about Sarah's age shouted and started to run after Lassie.

Two more little kids stood open-mouthed next to the bucket fire. Suddenly Lassie got in front of the running child and blocked her exit. The child, a girl of about five or six, crashed into the big collie.

Sarah suddenly knew the girl her age; she was in her fifth-grade class. What was her name? Something unusual? The smaller child screamed again, and Sarah flew over to Lassie. What was going on?

Lassie stood over the younger child, who had fallen down. She had one paw lightly on the child's shoulder, her silky white paw in the girl's red-gold hair. Terror filled the child's eyes and Sarah dropped to her knees beside her.

girl when Lassie pushed near again and swiped Imogene's face with her tongue.

Imogene giggled. Briny stared in shock at her. Lassie whined and suddenly rolled over, waving all four paws in the air. Imogene giggled again. "Funny dog," said Imogene.

"Silly dog," said Sarah. "What are you doing, Lassie?"

Briny said slowly, "She's showing my sister not to be scared."

"What?" asked Sarah.

"Scared. Imogene is terrified of dogs."

"This is a nice dog," said Imogene.

Lassie sat up and laughed, her long tongue flopping to her chest.

"I wouldn't believe it if I hadn't seen it," said Briny. But then her face hardened and she turned on Sarah. "What are you doing here?"

Sarah instantly felt guilty. "Nothing," she stammered. "I mean, we saw the smoke and wondered if the barn was burning."

"Well, it's not," stated Briny.

As if I couldn't figure that out, thought Sarah, her rising anger searing away the guilt.

"So, leave, okay?" said Briny.

Sarah was flabbergasted. How dare she?

Imogene had scrambled up, and Lassie stood pressed against the child, as if reassuring her.

"Excuse me," said Sarah in a poison-polite voice, "but you are trespassing."

"We aren't either," said Briny fiercely. "This property belongs to my mother. And until it's sold, it is ours. So double excuse you. You're trespassing."

Sarah started to say, "Triple excuse me," but just said instead, "We're leaving now." She whistled for Lassie and walked back around the barn. In the tall, late afternoon shadow, she realized Lassie had not come.

She whistled again, sharper. Still no Lassie. Sarah stomped around the corner again. The little girl had put her arms around Lassie's neck. The other children—another girl younger than Briny, and a boy, older than Imogene—had come close and were touching Lassie. The littlest boy had thrown his arms around the collie following his older sister's lead, his eyes closed in fierce concentration.

"Please let her stay," said Imogene softly.

Briny's eyes flashed as if she were going to snap out another command, but instead she covered her mouth with her hand. Sarah wasn't sure if Briny was going to laugh or cry.

A Deep Sadness

Briny laughed. And with her laughter all the children smiled. Even Sarah, though feeling foolish, grinned too.

"I'm sorry," said Briny after they'd disentangled the little girl. "You surprised us. And Imogene has been deadly afraid of dogs ever since one bit her when she was about Corey's age." Briny pointed to the littlest boy.

Imogene still had a hand on Lassie. "What is your dog's name?" she asked. "Lasso?"

"It's Lassie," Sarah replied. At her name the collie turned to Sarah, wagging her tail.

"She's a good dog," stated Imogene.

"She is," said Sarah. "She'll always be your friend."

"Always?" asked Imogene.

"Always," repeated Sarah, feeling as if she were making some kind of sacred vow for Lassie.

Briny said suddenly, "You're in my class."

"I know," said Sarah. "You're the one Mr. Jackson thinks isn't on earth."

Briny laughed again. "Isn't he awful?"

Sarah nodded happily. Mr. Jackson was strict and, in her professional opinion, gave way too much homework. "Did you finish that report? It wasn't fair that he moved up the deadline, was it?"

"I know," said Briny. "I had to stay up late to finish it."

"Me, too," said Sarah. She took off her jacket because the fire was hot.

The bucket flames gave a loud pop.

"Are these all your brothers and sisters?" asked Sarah. "You all look so much alike."

Briny introduced the others. "This is Gabby, she's nine, and Gus, he's seven."

"Nickname for Angus," said Gus, sitting down opposite Sarah and sinking his hands into Lassie's deep, rich coat. "I just love dogs," he said.

"Imogene's six and Corey is five," Briny continued, pointing to each child as she said his or her name.

"What are you guys doing here?" asked Sarah after a moment of quiet. No one answered right away. Sarah felt as if she'd bit down on a sore tooth. The fire crackled and popped again, adding to the tension of the silence. *I've put my foot in my mouth,* thought Sarah, but she didn't know why. Gabby started to stammer something about their mom's farm when Briny smoothly broke in.

"We're just playing house," she said, a little too brightly.

"You know, sort of pioneer kids. Our mom works late, so I try to entertain the kids."

Sarah really didn't know, being the youngest in her family and always having Mom around, but she knew when she was being put off track. So instead she asked, "Do you guys live around here, then?" She'd never seen Briny anywhere except school, which seemed sort of odd. Farley wasn't that big!

"Yeah, we live nearby," said Briny. Her brothers and sisters stared into the fire in silence. Imogene wrapped her arm around Lassie's neck, and the collie rested her slim muzzle in the child's lap.

"I live just over there," said Sarah, still trying to figure out what was going on. She hated feeling like everyone knew something, except her. "I live on the outskirts of town."

"Oh, yeah?" said Briny. "We live over there." She pointed the opposite direction from where Sarah had pointed and named a rural road about a mile from the farm.

"How come you don't live here since your family owns it?" asked Sarah. She had thought Dad said an old couple had owned it, but actually wasn't sure about her facts.

Briny shrugged. "Mom got tired of this place. It's alot of work, a farm. Our dad, um, isn't around and Mom couldn't keep up the farm."

"Yeah, it would be a lot of work," said Sarah. She

glanced around. Overgrown bushes crowded the boarded up house. The barn wasn't even fit for animals anymore. It wasn't like the olden days when kids stayed home and worked the farm. Sarah doubted one woman could run even a small farm without help. Maybe Briny's family was too poor to hire help.

In the dusky light, bats began to flit from the hayloft, searching for insects. Their high-pitched squeaks made Lassie prick her ears.

"I gotta get going," Sarah said suddenly, realizing it must be after five. She scrambled to her feet. "Mom's gonna kill me."

"Don't want that," said Briny, lightly. "See ya at school tomorrow." The kids called good-bye and scooted closer to the bucket fire. Gus tossed on some more sticks and twigs.

As Imogene hugged Lassie, saying, "Good-bye, friendly dog," Sarah wondered why the kids weren't heading home too. Even though it was spring, it was still cold at night. Sarah shivered. She decided to jog to keep warm, so she and Lassie followed the narrow path around the barn and out the way they'd come in.

On the slight rise, Sarah glanced behind her. The smoke had blended into the graying light, invisible. She thought, *Yeah, Briny, you should have waited until now to start your fire.* A deep sadness gripped her heart, but she didn't understand why.

No Troglodytes

The next day Jimmy and his ticket crew were to hold yet another meeting. This time they hoped to narrow down the suggestions for the events in the Wacky Rodeo. Eighth graders received the privilege of giving advice to the Farley rodeo committee since they were the oldest grade in their school. Jimmy and Katie had gone around to all the eighth graders' homeroom classes that day and asked the kids which events they liked most. Any new suggestions were gladly added to the list.

"Let's have the meeting at Cal's house," suggested Katie, still suspicious of Cal's motives. Since Mrs. Brickley wasn't staying after school today, Katie thought it would be a good time to find out more about Cal.

A small panic appeared in Cal's eyes, but he said calmly, "It would be better if we met at someone else's house. My mom's been kind of sick."

Jimmy knew Katie well enough to know she wasn't going to give up until she found out something more about

Cal, but Jimmy wasn't sure he liked her angle. "How about we meet at my house?" he said. Cal glanced at Jimmy. He wasn't sure what was in Cal's expression. Maybe relief? Thanks? But why? Cal was odd, but not in a bad way. All this was making Jimmy curious about the kid. It seemed as though Cal had a couple of secrets, and he wasn't telling them to anybody.

Having a pastor for a father, Jimmy knew that no one would be surprised to see extra people in the house. People were always stopping over to chat or counsel with his dad and mom. Jimmy liked it that way. He never felt afraid to invite his friends over.

"His mom makes the best cookies," said Blake as the four headed for Jimmy's house.

"You'll have to remind her of that," said Jimmy. "I think she's forgotten how to make them. She's been so busy doing other stuff."

❦

Sarah was already home when Jimmy, Katie, Blake, and Cal appeared. Lassie jumped up on Jimmy. She was as tall as Jimmy when she stood on her hind legs. She scoured his face with her tongue. "Cut it out," said Jimmy finally, laughing and pushing her back down.

"Nice dog. A collie, right?" said Cal. Jimmy nodded. Lassie politely sniffed Cal's outstretched hand. "My sisters and brothers met a collie like yours," said Cal. "My littlest sister is scared of dogs, but she liked the one she saw last night."

Sarah's head jerked up. "Where did your brothers and sisters meet the dog?"

"At my grandmother's farm," said Cal.

"That abandoned farm, by the pond?" asked Sarah.

Cal nodded, a little warily.

"That was me and Lassie. You do have a lot of brothers and sisters," she said, then added, "I thought Briny said the farm was your mom's?"

That small panic showed again in Cal's eyes. Sarah saw it and wondered.

"It belongs to my grandmother and our mother," Cal said. "You know, like a family farm."

"Cool," said Sarah, almost too quickly. "Too bad you guys can't live there and run it."

"Yeah," said Cal, not quite meeting her gaze. "Too bad."

"Enough chitchat," said Katie, apparently having heard enough about Cal for now.

Sheesh, girls! thought Jimmy. They couldn't make up their mind what they wanted.

"Let's get this list done," said Katie. "I have to work at the hardware store this afternoon or Granny will kill me."

Katie's grandmother, Rachel Madison, owned Madison's Hardware Store, and she expected Katie to spend a couple of afternoons a week helping out to do her fair share for the family business—with pay, of course.

The four sat at the kitchen table, Lassie at Jimmy's feet, while Sarah banged around in the kitchen.

"What events got the most votes?" asked Katie.

Jimmy slid a sheet of paper to Cal and Blake. "Add 'em up," he said. They counted as Sarah brought out soft drinks and a loaf of banana bread.

"Thanks, Sarah," said Jimmy. "Now what do you want?"

"Jimmy!" Both Sarah and Katie yelled, indignantly.

"What?" asked Jimmy.

"Can't Sarah be nice?" asked Katie.

"Yeah," said Sarah, her hands on her hips.

"She's never nice without a reason," said Jimmy. "And I speak from experience."

Sarah stuck out her tongue at her brother, then pulled up a chair and sat down. She reached for a slice of bread.

"Oh, no, you don't," said Jimmy. "This is for eighth graders only. Get lost."

"It's my house too," protested Sarah.

"So go to another part of *your* house."

"I want to be here!"

"Sarah!"

"Jimmy!"

Lassie barked and pawed Jimmy's leg.

Katie laughed. "It's Counselor Dog at work," she explained to Cal. "Lassie doesn't let this family get mad at each other without trying to make peace."

Cal grinned. "I like that."

Jimmy and Sarah glared at each other. Lassie barked again.

"Come on, you guys," said Katie. "Knock it off or she'll bark all afternoon."

Jimmy wasn't going to allow his little sister to hang out with them. He said through clenched teeth, "Get out of here, Sarah."

They stared at each other a long moment, until Sarah broke the gaze.

"Fine," she said, and flounced out of the room. Lassie whined, and anxiously trotted back and forth between them. Sarah waved her hand. "Come on, Lassie. I guess I don't want to be here after all." She left the room and stomped outside, slamming the front door behind her.

"Sisters," said Cal, knowingly.

"Amen," said Jimmy.

"Hey, I'm a sister," protested Katie.

"Case in point," said Blake, who had two older sisters.

Katie took a swing at him, but he neatly ducked, nearly knocking off his glasses.

"Anyway, back to the Wacky Rodeo," said Jimmy.

The list of events was pretty much set. They were to decide which of the crazier events to use.

WACKY RODEO

- Bareback pony broncs
- Rope Race (Two riders hold a length of rope between them and can't drop it while they ride a pattern. The team that goes the fastest without letting go of the rope wins.)

- Needle-and-Thread Relay (Aim a shoelace at the eye in a wooden peg on a pole. Team with most shoelaces in eye wins.)
- Buddy Pick-Up (One rider stands on barrel. Horse and other rider gallop up. As they turn around barrel, the one on the barrel jumps onto horse and the two riders gallop back riding double.)
- Pony Races
- Hog Tying Contest for adults/Bag the Piglet for kids

The bike events for anyone were:
- Trick Riding on Bikes
- Relay on Bikes
- Sand Surfing with Bikes
- Race Course with Tricycles

"I think this is gonna be the best Wacky Rodeo yet," declared Katie after she read the winning events out loud. "I like the pony races. I want to do that one."

"I like watching the guys chase that greased pig and try to get it to the ground," Blake said.

"I just hope we sell the most tickets," Jimmy added. "I want to meet Blair Coughlin and get his autograph, maybe even have my picture taken with him."

"Me, too," said Blake. "Did you see the game between the Cobras and the Bengals?"

"I did. Remember in the last quarter when Blair almost dropped the ball? He got hit so hard, they said it was like being struck by a car moving twenty miles an hour."

Katie slammed shut her notebook. "Guys, the purpose is to raise money for KidsTown, not to meet some troglodyte football player."

Jimmy, Blake, and Cal exchanged looks. Jimmy was horrified. Blair Coughlin was hardly the typical jock. He was a real thinker. Some of his football plays were classic. Girls! What did they know?

"Hey," said Blake. "Blair Coughlin was a foster kid at KidsTown. He got a football scholarship at USC—that's the University of Southern California, in case you didn't know. He was an awesome college player."

"So?" said Katie. "Lots of people go to college."

Blake groaned and put his head in his arms.

Jimmy had watched videos of Blair's early games. Even he could see why Blair was a first-round draft choice of the Cobras. Jimmy just sighed. Katie would never understand that Blair Coughlin was not just an Iowan, just any ole kid. He was a regular kid who made good. He made it to the big time. It gave a person hope that someday he or she might make it good too.

Jimmy couldn't put into words how he felt, so he said, "We better go sell some tickets."

Almost an Accident

That afternoon Sarah and Lassie had to return to the barn despite the falling rain. Sarah realized too late that she had forgotten her jacket by the fire. Last night Mom had asked her where it was when she'd come in shivering. Sarah hadn't known what to say. She didn't want to lie, but if she said she'd left it at the old barn, she'd get in trouble for being where she shouldn't be. She felt panicky inside. Sarah coughed to give herself a moment to think. Finally, she said she left her jacket in her school locker.

Now she had to get it.

When Sarah first entered the barn, she and Lassie both shook the rain from their hair. Gabby was wearing her jacket. It was too big for the younger girl, and when Gabby saw Sarah, she immediately tore it off.

"Nice jacket," Gabby said. She wore a thin, long-sleeved t-shirt. "I was just trying it on. I think I'll get one like it."

In that one moment Sarah knew the girl had been wearing it since yesterday.

Briny's head appeared at the the top of the hayloft. "Hey, Sarah, what are you doing here? Come on up," she called. So Sarah put on her jacket and climbed up the ladder.

"I had to come back for my jacket," Sarah said as she made her way up the ladder.

Sarah and Briny sat silently on bales in the hayloft. Sarah found a twist of baling wire in the dusty straw. She bent the wire to form a little horse. Well, at least she meant it to look like a horse. Mostly it looked like a bent piece of wire.

"How come you're so quiet?" Briny asked.

"Ah, I don't know," Sarah said. "Well, really I do know. I had to lie about where I left my jacket. I'm not allowed to be out here by this old barn, and if my mom found out I was here, she'd be mad."

"So, what's a little lie?" Briny said. "Who's going to know the difference?"

"I will!" Sarah replied. *And God will know too,* Sarah thought. "I don't like telling lies," she said matter-of-factly.

Sarah looked over at Corey who was sleeping between two bales of hay. He had a faded blue blanket wrapped around him. He looked so peaceful that Sarah wished she could be Corey's age again, when life was a whole lot less complicated.

Down below Lassie barked playfully. Briny and Sarah peered over the edge to see what was going on. Imogene had cowered a little when Sarah and Lassie had popped into the barn, but Lassie had walked over to her and laid down, placing her slim muzzle over her outstretched paws. As Imogene stroked the collie's drying coat, she looked up and said, "She feels like ribbons I had on a dress, smooth and soft."

Gus and Gabby started playing a sort of tag. Lassie quickly joined in. Imogene climbed up on the top panel of a stall divider, cheering them on. She had dropped an old tattered horse blanket over her shoulders.

"I saw your brother today," Sarah told Briny. Even with her jacket on, Sarah felt chilled. No fire crackled in the metal bucket or anywhere else. All the kids had to stay in the barn because of the rain. It was a dismal day.

A large drop fell on Sarah's nose.

"If you aren't careful you'll get just as wet in here," Briny said. A half a dozen leaks trickled into expanding pools on the barn floor. The two girls peered over the edge of the loft and watched the falling drops for a moment. "So which brother did you see?" asked Briny.

"Cal. Is he the oldest?" asked Sarah. For all she knew the Freedmans had even more siblings.

"Yeah," said Briny. "But Cal's enough, believe me. As bossy as he is."

"He seemed nice enough."

Briny shrugged and grinned. "He's okay, really. Where did you meet him?"

"At my house. I guess he's still there. He's part of the ticket selling team for KidsTown. My brother's the captain."

Briny transformed. She shifted into a stiff, prickly person, her relaxed, golden self, submerged somewhere. Briny nodded stiffly as if her neck hurt. "Cal mentioned it." End of subject.

Okay, whatever, thought Sarah. She was learning that certain areas were off limits. If she pushed the conversation, Briny would simply walk away and ignore her. Sarah didn't want that to happen.

"Let's make walls with the hay bales," she suggested after a long moment. "We can make rooms, like a house."

The golden glow returned to Briny's face, and together the girls shoved and heaved on the dusty bales, shifting them around the sleeping Corey.

Sarah sneezed five times in a row. "This stuff is nasty," she said. "Maybe we should let some rain get on it."

"Ick," said Briny. "Wet straw is gross. Anyway once we finish moving them, we won't touch 'em again." Briny answered Sarah's sneezes with some of her own.

Down below, Lassie barked happily, chasing one kid, then another. Imogene shouted and kicked her heels against the wooden divider. Sarah paused, leaning on the splintering rail to watch. She smiled, glad Lassie that had helped Imogene.

Gabby hopped up on an old goat-milking table and

rattled the metal stanchion. Nimbly Lassie sprang up behind her and bumped her with her wet nose.

"She tagged you!" shouted Gus. "Gabby's it now."

"Hey, I wasn't playing right then," protested Gabby. "I was looking at this thing."

As if she understood, Lassie leaped away, barking.

"You're it," yelled Imogene, the self-appointed referee.

So, good-naturedly, Gabby sprang off the table and charged after Gus and Lassie. Gus took off across the barn floor, and Lassie jumped back up onto the table. Then she disappeared around a corner.

Sarah chuckled. Honestly, Lassie was acting practically like another kid, a kid with lots of fur. Sarah was just about to call down something about Lassie being a fur kid when a loud crack shot through the barn.

Something slammed into Sarah, knocking her down. She sprawled on the loft floor. A sharp pain stabbed her left shoulder.

For a frozen second, the silence was louder than the rocketing report. Then Gus, Gabby, and Imogene began hollering. Lassie barked her deep warning. Corey woke and cried.

Lassie rolled off of Sarah. She had knocked Sarah down.

"Why did you do that?" asked Sarah and she sat up, rubbing her shoulder. "You hurt me." Lassie whined and nuzzled her.

"You would have been hurt worse if she hadn't snuck up the ladder," snapped Briny. "Look at the rail."

Sarah looked. A good five feet of the wooden rail had broken off and fallen below.

Gabby's head popped up from the top of the ladder. "Gosh, are you okay?"

Briny's face had gone white. Slowly color crept back into it. Sarah wondered if her face looked as white.

Still rubbing her shoulder, Sarah stood and examined the shattered railing. The barn floor was a good fifteen foot drop. Sarah looked stupidly from Briny to Lassie, not knowing what to say.

Briny held out her hands. "Look. I'm shaking." Her fingers trembled.

Sarah turned to her and held the other girl's hands. "If I'd fallen—" She didn't want to think what could have happened. She put her arms around Lassie.

Below Gus picked up the rail and brandished it like a sword. Sarah began to wonder how much of the wood was decaying. A swirl of dizziness took her and she had to sit down. "Maybe we shouldn't be up here," said Sarah. "What if more of the wood is bad?"

Briny had been holding Corey so he would stop crying. His nose kept running though. Briny said, "Cal told me the loft was sound enough. He did say the railing was going. I forgot that. I'm really sorry, Sarah."

"It's okay," said Sarah. "I should have thought it might be weak."

How had Lassie known? wondered Sarah.

Outside the rain slowed. Heavy, slow drops tumbled from the pitched roof to the various widening pools of water on the floor bottom. Imogene had slid off the stall divider and was busy sweeping at the water with a makeshift broom.

When Lassie carefully went back down the ladder to play, Sarah said, slowly, almost to herself, "You guys live here, don't you?"

Briny started to protest. Sarah just stared at her until Briny said in a small voice, "Don't tell anyone, Sarah, please."

Sarah's Secret Plan

At dusk Sarah and Lassie headed home. What was she going to tell Mom she had been doing? Taking long walks? Why? Mom would ask. Because she felt like it? Because she wanted to get in better shape? Somehow she didn't think Mom would buy those answers.

Sarah thought. Maybe she could tell Mom she was looking for some material for a nature collage. Even in the rain? Well, it began raining after she'd been gone a while.

The nature collage was the best she could think of, so she hastily stuffed her jacket pockets with damp leaves, a bunch of flowers, and a couple of milkweed pods.

Mom definitely would not approve of her playing in the abandoned barn. And if she knew that six kids lived there—Sarah wondered how far Mom's compassion would go. She was afraid it wouldn't spread too thick.

She and Lassie hopped over a couple of stones the size of a soccer ball. Too bad they weren't closer to the barn. Before she left the kids, she helped Briny and Gabby carry smooth, round stones inside the barn so they could have their fire inside out of the rain.

"Be careful," Sarah had warned. "This barn would make a mega bonfire."

Briny nodded. "We will."

"Why did you choose this barn?" Sarah asked.

"It was close to our schools," Briny said. "No one is around here. We were in foster homes a couple of times before, and they separated us. Cal and I were in one home; Gabby, Imogene and Gus in another; and poor Corey was all alone in another home.

Then she asked Sarah again, "You won't tell, will you?"

Sarah shook her head. "I promise I won't." But her heart lay heavy inside her, like one of the fire stones.

"I can't blame them for wanting to stay together, can you?" Sarah asked Lassie as they crossed the two-lane road behind the Harmon's property. "I wouldn't want to be separated from you or Jimmy if something happened to Mom and Dad." But a lot of the time, grown-ups didn't seem to care what kids wanted.

Sarah opened the back door and walked inside to the tangy smell of ginger. "Yum," she said, poking her head in the kitchen.

Mom started to smile at her, then she said sternly, "Where have you been, young lady? You look like you've been sitting in a mud hole."

Sarah pulled out a handful of damp leaves and flowers. "Looking for nature stuff. I'm going to do a collage." Her words tasted like dust. Lying was awful. She had to stop.

"For heaven's sakes, Sarah. Go wash up and change out of those clothes. Lassie looks cleaner than you do."

Obediently, Lassie had paused in the entrance way on the tile floor, waiting for her paws to be wiped. Mom grabbed a rag and cleaned the collie's paws. "Where have you two been?" Mom asked the dog.

Good thing Lassie couldn't talk! Just then Sarah had a fabulous idea! She ran up the stairs, taking the steps two at a time.

※

That night after dinner, Jimmy sat at the kitchen table counting the ticket money with nervous fingers. Each morning Pastor Harmon would take the cash and checks from the previous day's sales to the bank. Everyone agreed that a pastor was the most trustworthy person to do the job. He would deposit the money into a special account set up for the eighth-grade class. All the money would go to KidsTown after the rodeo.

"Well, son, do you have the deposit ready for tomorrow morning?" Paul Harmon asked as he went to the refrigerator for a refill of iced tea.

"Yes, Dad," Jimmy responded. "I've counted and recounted the money."

"Good, I'd hate to get up to the teller window at the bank and have the wrong amount," Pastor Harmon replied.

"Yeah, I guess that would look pretty bad for a pastor, especially if you said you had more money than you actually had."

Sarah came down the stairs to get some clothes out of the dryer. When she heard Jimmy and Dad talking, she stopped to listen from the stairwell.

Dad reached for a couple of cookies from the cookie jar. "We have to be careful not to jump to conclusions that aren't true. Anyone can make an honest mistake."

"You know what I mean, Dad," Jimmy said.

"The truth of the matter is, Jim," his dad continued, "it doesn't matter who you are or what you do, whether you're a doctor, truck driver, or pastor. Every person has to answer to God for his or her own actions. We have to ask ourselves, 'How does my life line up against what God tells us in His Word that we should do? Are we honest, truthful, responsible, full of integrity?' "

Sarah felt sick. She had made so many bad choices lately, so many things she wished she could do over. She didn't even want to think about what God might think at this point. Sarah turned and went back upstairs. She'd heard all she wanted to for now.

Dad took a big bite of a cookie. "These are the things that show the world that God has the power to change a life. Otherwise, left to our sinful nature, who knows what kind of person we'd be."

"I see what you mean," Jimmy said. "We become a witness to our friends even if we aren't trying to be."

"Something like that," Dad said. "Well, I'm going to head to bed. I'll see you in the morning."

"Yeah, me, too," Jimmy said. He gathered up all of his stuff and headed for his bedroom. He decided to count the money again just to be sure.

He wondered if he had enough sales to win so he could meet Blair Coughlin? *Please, God, please, please, please.* What did God do when a bunch of kids prayed for the same thing and only a few could have their prayer answered the way they wanted?

Lassie lay flat on her side next to him, her legs stretched straight out. She was snoring lightly. Jimmy counted softly under his breath, "Fifty-six, fifty-eight, sixty dollars."

Today he had one hundred and eight dollars in cash and twenty-six dollars in checks. Not all of it was from his personal sales. Mrs. Brickley, his homeroom teacher, gave him the money each day from eighth-grade students who sold tickets the day before.

Carefully he wrote the amounts in a ledger. Mrs. Brickley double-checked his addition. So far he didn't have any mistakes. When he was done, he carefully put the money in the two-foot-tall ceramic collie bank sitting on his desk.

A knock fell on his closed bedroom door. Before he answered the door, he started to slide the ceramic collie under his bed, then felt foolish. As if anyone in his family would take the ticket money. He left it on his desk.

"Come," he said, making himself not say come in. "Come" sounded very starshiplike. He liked that thought.

Sarah opened his door. Lassie sat up and yawned, her long pink tongue a raspberry ribbon down her chest. "Can I come in?" Sarah asked.

Jimmy was feeling friendly. "Sure."

She came in and shut the door behind her. She twisted her hands together in front of her and asked, "Do you have any old shirts or pants you don't want any more?"

He stared at her. "Why? You need a new wardrobe?"

"Very funny," she snapped. "I'm gonna take some stuff to, you know, the Salvation Army tomorrow and I wondered if you had anything you wanted to get rid of."

Jimmy shrugged. "Probably." He opened a drawer in his dresser and rummaged through t-shirts. He tossed a couple to her.

"Any pants?" she asked. "Socks?" She sounded desperate, or something.

He shot her a look. "What is this?"

She hesitated as if she were going to say something, but instead she closed up and just said, "For Salvation Army. They can use pants and socks." He knew she had

52

some other reason, but he couldn't think what in the world it would be.

So he shrugged and said, "Whatever." He knew the drill. At least once a year the Harmons plowed through unused clothes and stuff to be given away. Mom always said, "We have too much junk. Our possessions possess us!"

Jimmy opened another drawer, then slid open his closet. He poked around, then gave her a pair of jeans, too small in the waist, and a pair of brown cords that were too short. He eyed his sister a moment. "Are you getting rid of all your clothes so Mom will buy you new stuff?"

"No!"

She had done that last year. Was Mom mad at Sarah! Jimmy still couldn't think of any other reason. "Want some underwear?" he asked. He pulled some old cartoon character boxer shorts over his head and grinned at her out one leg hole.

Without a word, Sarah snatched the boxers off his head. She gathered up the rest of his clothes and sailed out of his room, slamming his door.

Lassie jumped and whined anxiously.

"Don't ask me," he said to the dog. "She's going nutzo." Jimmy dropped back onto his bed. *Sisters! Sheesh!*

Lying to the Sheriff

The next day after school, Sarah carried a paper shopping bag stuffed with clothes from Jimmy and herself. In her backpack, she had taken food from their pantry. Again, no one had been home, so she helped herself to mostly canned stuff. It weighted about ten tons.

She and Lassie hiked across the field. The sheep were gone today. Too bad people couldn't graze like horses and sheep. Food would certainly be easier to get.

Sarah had also loaded Lassie's dog pack and made the collie carry bags of noodles, rice, dried soup, and one of Mom's old cooking pots. She hoped Mom wouldn't miss it for a while.

Ladened down, Sarah and Lassie strode into the quiet barnyard. Where were the kids? They wouldn't be inside, would they? It wasn't raining today. "Briny," she started to call, when Lassie growled low in her throat.

Sarah glanced around, still seeing no one, but Lassie continued to growl, menacingly.

"Is someone here?" Sarah's voice quavered and she instantly regretted speaking.

From behind a sycamore tree beside the barn, a man stepped out. A man in a sheriff's uniform. "What are you doing here?" he demanded.

Guilt exploded through Sarah. She shouldn't feel guilty, should she? She wasn't doing anything wrong, was she?

Another part of her mind spit out information as if not even connected to her:

You are trespassing, Sarah.

You are helping kids to live without grown-ups.

You took food from your house without asking.

Wait, she protested. Would a sheriff care about the food she carried? She didn't think so.

She answered him, trying to keep her voice even, "I'm just walking, to, to get in shape." Lassie had quit growling at his voice as if she knew what he represented. She sat, her tail spread behind her like a Persian rug, the red dog packs bulging with goods.

"Just walking around," repeated the sheriff. "Not running away?"

"No!" Too late Sarah realized how it must look to him. "I'm not running away, really. You can, can follow me home, if you like. I'm just getting ready to turn back."

"I bet you are." His face was expressionless, but his tone made her flush with embarrassment.

She wasn't doing anything wrong!

Was she?

"Did you know this was private property?" he asked.

"Well, actually, yes," she said, trying not to lie unless she had to. *That sounded bad,* she thought. But she wasn't doing anything wrong. Just helping Briny and the kids. Sarah stumbled on, "But no one lives here, right? So I just come through here on my way to the pond and stuff."

"The pond and stuff."

She hated the way he repeated her words, making her feel like a liar and an idiot at the same time.

He stood before her like a giant, bulging arm muscles folded across his chest. She couldn't keep her eyes off the gun around his waist. He said, "I'm here because neighbors have reported seeing a bunch of kids hanging around where they shouldn't be." He reached down and flicked off dried mud from his black boot. He continued, "In addition to this being private property, this old barn is dangerous. It's no place to play."

Sarah thought unwillingly of yesterday and the spilt railing. He must have been inside the barn. She couldn't understand how the kids had escaped being seen.

"Have you seen kids around here?" he asked. "While you're walking to get in shape?"

She shook her head no. *At least not today,* she thought. That was the truth.

"Isn't this Pastor Harmon's dog?" he asked suddenly.

Oh great, she groaned inwardly. If he were to tell Dad that he'd seen her here, she'd been in deep muck. No, she reminded herself, I'm just out walking, remember? It's a free country. I can take a walk when I want.

"Yes, sir," said Sarah. "This is Lassie, his family dog. And I'm Pastor Harmon's daughter, Sarah Harmon."

The sheriff stared hard into her eyes. Surely he could tell she was holding back information! But all he said was, "Aye, Sarah, do us a favor and stay off this property, all right?"

She swallowed hard and nodded, to show she heard him, but she had one hand at her side and she crossed her fingers. Lassie allowed the sheriff to stroke her, and she even wagged her tail.

Then he turned and walked away toward the house and the road where his car rested under an elm tree. Sarah figured she was dismissed and fled as fast as she could walk, certain he watched her until she was out of sight. She was too scared to even turn around to check.

She reached the edge of the pond and the circle of weeping willows. She parted the hanging limbs with their tiny green leaves and finally felt safe, unseen. After a moment to catch her breath, she stored the food that wasn't canned up in one of the weeping willows near the pond. She took off Lassie's packs, then stuffed them completely full with the other packages. Standing on a rock, she wedged the dog pack high up on a limb so no animal could reach it. The clothes she put in a tight bundle behind a large stone and covered them with the canned goods. Then she tossed handfuls of leaves over the pile, hoping no one would come by and take them before she could tell Briny and the kids about it.

Tomorrow at school she would tell Briny. She didn't dare leave a note in fear someone would find it and take the stuff. Or the sheriff would find it and know Pastor Harmon's daughter had lied to him.

Even though only Lassie was with her, she still blushed red to think that she had just lied to an officer. Mom and Dad wouldn't be happy if they knew. In fact, they wouldn't be happy about a lot of things she was doing lately.

But she had to help Briny. She couldn't let the kids starve or get split up. She had to do what she had to do.

The Heat Is On

After school, Jimmy climbed onto the rodeo fence. Before long he would see Blair Coughlin of the Colorado Cobras. During homeroom the assistant principal announced over the intercom that the seventh and eighth grades were running close firsts for ticket sales. He wouldn't say who had the most, but Jimmy was sure it was the eighth graders. Well, pretty sure.

"Would you play professional ball?" Jimmy asked Blake who was perched next to him on the fence.

"If I got asked, sure," said Blake. "Professional players make a lot of money. I wouldn't mind that!"

Cal was on the other side of the arena, poking around in the animal pens. He held up a horseshoe. "Good luck sign!" he called.

Jimmy and Cal exchanged a glance. Jimmy didn't think that Christians depended on luck, but he didn't want to sound mean to Cal. He raised a thumb in an "all right" signal.

Katie was with a Mrs. somebody-or-another from KidsTown. They were climbing the bleachers of the grandstand "to get a proper view." Jimmy knew Katie heard Cal by the way she stared long at him, but the KidsTown lady said something to her and she turned away. Katie probably would have blasted Cal about pagan rites or something. Katie was bold in the Lord, but sometimes not very tactful. Dad always told Jimmy that the Holy Spirit was a gentleman and that he ought to be too.

Blake continued with their conversation as if nothing had happened. "How 'bout you, Jim? You want to play professional ball?"

Jimmy shook his head ruefully. "I'm afraid I'd never make the cut. Maybe I'll run marathons or something."

"I think I want to go to med school," said Blake, "not end up being treated for medical problems."

"Blair Coughlin hasn't been injured much," said Cal. He had walked over with the horseshoe and climbed up on the fence beside Jimmy.

"Just wait," said Blake. "Give him a few years and he'll be arthritic. His sacroiliac will ache on cold days and his clavicles will be killing him."

"His what?" asked Cal.

"Do humans have sacroiliacs?" asked Jimmy.

Blake went on reciting various parts of the body where Blair Coughlin was sure to be hurting. *Show off*, thought Jimmy. He wondered if God called people to professional sports. He'd heard Blair Coughlin was a Christian and had read an interview with him in one of Dad's churchy magazines where he told how God helped him.

Jimmy wondered. Everyone talked about God calling people to be missionaries and pastors, but did God call people to be football players, baseball players, and soccer players? That sounded funny, but why not? Weren't you supposed to do everything as unto the Lord?

"Hey, Jimmy," hollered Katie from behind him. "Guess what? We can sell tickets over the phone! I got a mailing list of people and organizations all over Iowa who donate money to KidsTown!"

Jimmy jumped off the fence. "That's great, Katie!"

She ran over to join the guys, with her eyes shining, several pages in her hand. "We can start phoning tonight after five when the rates are lower, and look," she said as she read down the list. "Most of the organizations have toll free numbers."

"That's good," Blake said. "My dad doesn't mind buying a few tickets, but paying for a bunch of long distance calls . . . I don't know if he feels *that* generous."

Katie smiled. "It won't cost much, you'll see."

Katie is always so practical, Jimmy thought. He figured God would call Katie to a ministry where she would be something useful and organized.

She handed a page to each of them. But when she held one out to Cal, he didn't take it.

"We don't have a phone," said Cal quietly. "Sorry."

Katie stared at him like she didn't believe him.

"My dad has a second line at home for work," said Jimmy, quickly. "We might be able to call on it."

"But we are supposed to call after five?" asked Cal.

"Well, it's cheaper then," said Katie.

"I'm supposed to get home about then," said Cal. "My mom's rules, you know. Sorry."

"That's okay," Jimmy jumped in. "I can call his share. No problem."

Katie gave Cal a sharp look, but handed the page over to Jimmy.

Jimmy realized Katie thought Cal was being flaky or shirking his duty. Somehow he didn't think so. Cal seemed too real to be up to something.

"It's okay," said Jimmy quickly. "I can do a lot of calling tonight. I don't have much homework." He had some homework, but, hey, the ticket selling was as important as schoolwork. Well, more important!

❧

Sarah dragged home after dark. She had a headache and just wanted to lay down on cool, clean sheets in her bed. She opened the back door quietly, and she and Lassie slipped in. Her brother was on the phone in the kitchen, but he still hollered out, "Here's the prodigal daughter!"

Mom flew into the kitchen from the family room. "Sarah Elizabeth Harmon! Where have you been?"

Lassie crept under the kitchen table, her ears back, her tail down.

"Man, she looks guilty," remarked Jimmy. Then abruptly he said in a polished tone, "Good evening. This is James Harmon calling concerning KidsTown. How are you this evening?"

Sarah rolled her eyes at her brother's performance.

Mom repeated, "Where have you been?"

Sarah shrugged off her jacket and empty backpack. "Walked farther than I realized." She was lying again. How many times was that today? She didn't want to count.

"You haven't answered my question," said Mom. "Where were you?"

Jimmy, still speaking in his flowing, preacher tones, frantically waved at them to keep it down.

Mrs. Harmon took Sarah's elbow and led her into the guest bedroom next to the staircase. Lassie didn't follow. *Coward,* Sarah thought. She plopped onto the neatly made bed. The old starburst quilt had been made by Gram Harmon. It smelled of lavender. Sarah turned onto her stomach and buried her face in the soft material.

Should she tell Mom about Briny and the kids? She had promised Briny not to tell, but sometimes promises had to be broken. Yet Briny was so terrified that her family would be torn apart. Sarah couldn't tell, she just couldn't.

What if Sarah told Mom about the kids, then Mom told the authorities who then separated the kids? It would be all

Sarah's fault that they were divided. That would be like betrayal or high treason or something, wouldn't it?

She wondered if she could call KidsTown, anonymously, and ask about their policy of keeping families together. Would she be told the truth?

Sarah never used to worry so much about truth and lies. Now it seemed that one lie led to another, and she was beginning to feel trapped. What if she messed up and forgot how she had answered a question? It had all started so innocently, and now she had a real mess on her hands. She was just trying to protect Briny and her brothers and sisters. Surely God would understand that, wouldn't He?

She sighed and turned onto her back. "Mom, I was just walking with Lassie. We got farther than I realized. I'm sorry. I wasn't thinking."

Actually she had hung around the edges of the farm until dusk, hoping to see Briny, but she never did. What if the sheriff had already caught Briny and the kids? Already they might be a divided family and she was lying for no reason. She thought her brain was beginning to melt down; so much swirled inside her skull.

Mom stood without talking for a moment. Jimmy's voice droned on from the kitchen about the Wacky Rodeo, the tickets, how the money would help the kids. Sarah was getting very sick of the Wacky Rodeo. She was getting sick of everything!

"You know, Sarah," said Mom, slowly, "I've watched

you for many years now. I think I can tell when you're not telling me everything," said Mom.

That smarted. "Are you saying I'm lying?" she asked, glint appearing in her eyes.

"There is such a thing as half truth," said Mom.

"Meaning?"

"Meaning you aren't telling me everything."

"Mom," said Sarah firmly, sticking to her story. "There is nothing to tell except I took a walk. I walked too far. I got home late. I'm sorry. Can I go to the bathroom, please?"

Sarah wanted to run from the room before she burst into tears. She felt as though Mom could see right through to her heart.

Mom stood aside, her silence louder than any scolding or yelling. Sarah stalked into the small downstairs bathroom, closed the door and locked it. Since the toilet in this bathroom wasn't working very well, Mom would know yet again that Sarah was hiding something. She was acting very suspicious. Sarah turned on the cold water in the sink and splashed her face. She stared at her image in the mirror. She didn't like what she saw.

What's happening to me? she thought.

Secret Door

The next day at school during morning recess, Sarah ran up to Briny. In class she never had a chance to talk to Briny, and she was afraid to slip her a note because Monique was on one side of Briny, and Sarah knew Monique would read the note before passing it on, if she'd even pass it on. She was being a real stinker, like yesterday during math. Briny had been called up to figure one of those five story addition problems. Just then an office worker had called their teacher, Mrs. Austin, out into the hall.

As Briny walked to the blackboard, Monique had whispered loudly, "Doesn't she know ripped jeans are supposed to be fake ripped, not totally old and real ripped?"

Briny's neck and ears had turned red and Sarah had said coldly and just as loudly, "Some people care about people, not what they wear."

Monique had laughed cattily and said, "Sarah, the savior of misfits" just as Mrs. Austin stepped back into the room. The laughter and talk had stopped instantly, but

Briny's neck and ears remained red.

Sarah caught up to Briny at the edge of the playing field. "Where were you guys?"

Today Briny was wearing a cast-off flannel shirt of Sarah's and jeans with no tears, fake or not. "Hiding," Briny said.

Sarah opened her mouth at the sight of her shirt. She hadn't noticed it earlier in class. "How did you know?"

"I tracked you," said Briny. "You were easy to follow."

"How did you know what I had?"

Briny laughed, like golden tones. "Girl, you were so loaded down with stuff I can't understand why the sheriff didn't haul you in."

Could you be hauled in for carrying clothes and food? Sarah thought. *It's not like they were stolen or anything.* "But how did you see me?" Sarah persisted.

Briny winked. "We were hiding in the hay, and I was looking out the loft door."

"You're kidding," said Sarah.

"Everybody crowded into the trapdoor."

"Trapdoor?" exclaimed Sarah. "Where?"

Briny's eyes shone. "Two nights ago, Gus was playing around in the loft, sweeping some of the old hay and dust and he found this rope. It was tied to a ring of iron in the floor; or what he thought was the floor of the hayloft. It was really a trapdoor into a small room."

"A secret room," whispered Sarah. "Your family didn't know about it?"

"How could they?" asked Briny.

Puzzlement crossed Sarah's face. "Wouldn't your family know? Didn't they build the barn?"

"Oh, that. I guess they forgot to tell us kids."

Suddenly Sarah knew Briny had lied to her. The farm didn't belong to her mother or her grandmother or anyone else in her family. But why would Briny lie to her about the farm?

Because she and the kids had nowhere else to go.

"Anyway, thanks for the clothes and food," said Briny. "We had a great dinner last night."

"You're welcome," said Sarah.

Last night Mom had been in the pantry and had said, "I thought I had a couple of bags of noodles. When did we use those, Sarah?"

She had swallowed and said, "I don't know, Mom." But she did know. She knew she had taken them out to the farm with the other food supplies.

Briny pulled Sarah close and said, "Tomorrow is Gus's birthday. Do you think you could get him a cake or something?"

"I'm not sure." Poor kid, to have a birthday and no cake or party or anything. Could she make a cake? What could she tell Mom she was making it for? Briny looked sad. "I'll see what I can do," Sarah promised.

✣

Jimmy's PE class suited up and for fifteen minutes watched a video of the Colorado Cobras scrimmage. Of course, Blair Coughlin was front and center. The rugged, tan face of number 42 called out the play, neatly took the snapped pigskin, then delivered a perfect pass.

"This guy is great," said Coach Myler. "Look at that pass. It's beautiful."

"Everything is beautiful to you, Coach, . . . compared to us," said an eighth grader. A bunch of kids laughed, but Jimmy sat with his eyes fixed on what was happening on the screen.

"Harmon," snapped Coach Myler. "You think you're smart enough to make a pass like that?"

"At a girl," intoned some clown.

Everyone cracked up again and Jimmy grinned. "I'm a runner, Coach, not a great pass thrower," Jimmy said.

"Well, listen up all of you wanna-bes, and maybe you'll learn something about football," the coach said quickly, hoping to slide over Jimmy's lack of enthusiasm.

Jimmy sighed to himself as the coach rewound the video and played back the pass again. It would be beautiful to meet Blair Coughlin. Get his autograph. He hoped he could get his photo taken with number 42. He'd blow the photo up to poster size and hang it on his bedroom wall.

"Coughlin makes football playing an art," Coach Myler went on. Number 42 wound in and out of the attacking defense and evaded them. Then he threw a clean pass. "Just beautiful," breathed Coach.

"Is that the only adjective the coach knows?" someone whispered.

The kid next to Jimmy said, "He knows a lot of them, but you can't say them in school."

The video ended with Blair Coughlin yanking off his helmet and giving a thumbs up sign. Jimmy gave the thumbs up sign back to Blair's grin. *I'll sell the most tickets, Blair*, he told number 42 silently as the video stopped. *Just watch and see if I don't.*

After school, Jimmy and Sarah argued in the Harmon's kitchen. "You've had Lassie every day for the last week," Jimmy told Sarah. "It's time that I take over from here on. I want to put a sign on Lassie about the rodeo tickets. Maybe we'll get some more sales."

Sarah knew that was true. She'd been hogging Lassie. She guessed she could meander over toward the abandoned barn today alone. Briny had told her at afternoon recess that she'd show her the trapdoor. Maybe it would be just as well if Lassie stayed behind. She was going to buy a cake or something for Gus's birthday. Baking a cake at home would be too complicated.

So Sarah tossed her hair over her shoulder in a smug way and went upstairs. She shut her bedroom door and took down the special jewelry box she'd gotten when her family had gone to a theme park a couple of years ago. Underneath the purple, velvet-lined bottom was a shallow space where she kept her money. She had exactly twelve dollars. She smoothed the rumpled five dollar bill. She had been saving to get some fashion doll stuff, but it was better to give than to receive, wasn't it? . . . That's what her dad said.

Slowly she smoothed out the rest of her money—another five and two one dollar bills—and shoved them into her jeans pocket. Then before she could change her mind, she hurried down the stairs. As she was shutting the front door, she heard Jimmy call, "Now where is Lassie's dog pack?"

Sarah clicked shut the front door and ran to the store.

Barn Birthday

After going to the store, Sarah ran to the outskirts of town and out to the barn. As she opened the barn door, Briny called to her from the loft.

"Come on up," she yelled from above. Sarah quickly climbed the ladder. When Sarah reached the top, Briny opened the secret door. Sarah stared down into the trap-door space. Old blankets and towels padded the wooden slats. It was smaller than she had imagined, only about the size of her closet if it were laying down instead of upright. No one, even the littlest, Corey, could stand or even sit upright inside with the door shut.

"It's scary in there when the door is closed," said Imogene.

Sarah believed her. "Is that where you were yester-day?" asked Sarah. She knew it was, but Imogene nod-ded, wide-eyed.

"If Lassie could stay with me, I wouldn't be scared," said Imogene shyly.

Briny carefully shut the trapdoor. "Last night the kids stayed down there," said Briny. "But I left the door open part way."

Sarah glanced at Briny. "Did the sheriff come back again?" she asked.

"We were afraid he would," said Briny, "so Cal and I took turns watching out the hole in the wall."

What a life. "Hey, I have a surprise for a certain birthday boy," said Sarah. Gus's face lit up.

"Me?" he asked.

"Anyone else here having a birthday?" asked Briny with a grin. They made Gus go down the ladder. "No peeking," commanded Briny. "I'd tell him to go outside, except, you know, someone might call the cops again."

Sarah slipped off her backpack and unzipped it. All the kids except Gus crowded around. She pulled out a package of chocolate filled sandwich cookies, the kind with a hole in the middle. She whispered so Gus couldn't hear, "I was afraid a cake would get smashed in my backpack." Actually the cakes in the grocery bakery were expensive.

She had used almost all of her money anyhow. She pulled out a pack of rainbow-colored birthday candles. "We can stick a candle in a cookie hole," she explained. So she and Briny lined up eight cookies, since that was how old Gus was, and stuck a candle in each one.

"We'll light them tonight," said Briny. "You can see them

73

better then." Then the two girls divided up the rest of the cookies into little piles so that everyone could have an equal share of the party loot.

Sarah pulled out a plastic bag of toy cowboys and Indians, a coloring book of heavy equipment and trucks, and a box of sixteen crayons. "Double his age," she explained. They stuffed the toys in the paper bag from the store and neatly folded it shut. Sarah wished she had thought to get a little wrapping paper and ribbon.

Briny's eyes glittered in the late afternoon light. "This is so nice of you," she said, her voice a little choked. Sarah had noticed the kids didn't have any toys with them, not even little Corey.

"Ready?" Gus called from below.

"No!" hollered Briny and Sarah together. Gus laughed, dancing in place and hugging himself.

Sarah had also bought a bag of assorted soft candies. Gabby brought them an old metal bucket, turned it over, and Sarah set the bag of candies on it. She also had a carton of milk and a six-pack of cold Cokes.

"Your pack must have weighed a ton," said Gabby.

"It did."

They lined up the eight cookies and candles on a wobbly, wooden stool, along with the little piles of cookies.

Sarah pulled a bunch of bananas and a bag of apples from her bag. Briny carefully placed the fruit in a wooden crate behind a bale of hay. She came back with a strand of baling wire and twisted it into a circle. Then she reached over and slid the barrette out of Sarah's long hair.

"Hey!" Sarah said, not really realizing what Briny was doing. Her barrette was new, shiny with gold beads and red plastic stars, and she didn't want to see it get ruined.

Briny clipped the barrette to the wire circle. "A birthday crown," she said.

"Oh, okay," said Sarah, laughing. Briny was clever. Finally they called Gus. He flew up the ladder.

Briny carefully set the crown on his head. She curtsied to him. He grinned and clapped his hands.

They sang "Happy Birthday," with Gus bellowing to himself. He danced in circles, his crown slipping down, and the old loft shuddered under his jumps. Sarah was glad when he calmed down.

Everyone ate their stack of cookies, all but the candle-decorated eight. Sarah gave most of her cookies to the other kids. She could eat cookies most any day. They passed the milk around and drank straight from the carton.

Gus played with his toy figures. Corey grabbed the crayons and began coloring. "Only two pages," Gus told him. "The rest are mine." Corey stuck out his lip and immediately began coloring the splintering wood walls.

After the party, Sarah made sure she got home early. The kitchen clock read four. Mom wasn't even home. Dad was at church. Jimmy was gone, and she was glad.

She flopped onto her bed. Sarah wished she could do more for the kids. But how? The five of them had eaten so much in just such a short time. And Cal wasn't even there. He was the oldest and biggest. He probably ate a lot.

I've used all my money, too, she thought. She double-checked her jewelry box just in case, but found nothing but a couple of plastic beads. *Too bad they aren't real gems,* she thought. *I could sell them if they were diamonds or something.*

Sarah wandered downstairs and poked around in the pantry. She took a few more cans of soup and a jar of applesauce. Mom would be really suspicious if she took anymore. Mom was already trying to figure out where some of the food had gone. How could Sarah get food for the kids?

Too bad the people in their church put offerings into a wooden box in the back of the chapel. She could have taken some of the offering if they passed it around in baskets or plates.

Then she remembered her parents kept a vase with silk sunflowers in their bedroom. The clear vase was half dark with change.

Sarah scooted upstairs. She tossed the cans into her backpack, then thrust it under her bed. She went into her parents' room. The windows faced west, looking out on the backyard. The sun was a circle of fire sliding down. The walls in her parents' room were painted a lively green and yellow; it seemed like a garden. The vase rested on the round table that held the phone. Sarah pulled the silk sunflowers out and laid them on the bed.

I'll just take quarters, she decided as she lifted out a handful of rattling change. She picked out seven quarters and dumped the other change back into the jar. She dug deep into the heavy coins and lifted out another handful. Five more quarters. Then she drew out two more handfuls until she had nearly eight dollars in quarters.

Downstairs the front door slammed. She jumped, but swiftly replaced the sunflowers in the vase. Holding the quarters tightly in her hands, she darted out of her parents' room and into her own. She closed the door.

More Surprises for Sarah

The day after the birthday, Sarah had to go to the orthodontist. "Braces soon, Sarah," the dentist had told her. Once that had been upsetting, but now she had more important things to worry about.

So the following day, Sarah and Lassie paid a visit to Briny and the kids at the barn. Imogene would be so disappointed if Lassie didn't come again. Sarah couldn't bear the thought of having to explain to Imogene that she couldn't bring Lassie every time. Jimmy was getting a little suspicious of Sarah's wanting to take Lassie out for exercise all the time. Sarah would have to be careful.

Sarah and Lassie found the kids downstairs, eating slices of bologna and American cheese. "Where did you get that?" asked Sarah. She hadn't bought them.

Briny winked. "I have my ways."

Sarah wondered. She unpacked the pantry food and the food she'd bought with the vase quarters early before school at the 24-hour grocery store. With all her own money gone, and the quarters gone, she'd have to dip into the vase a second time unless she could think of another way to get food or money.

If only she could talk to Dad or one of the elders. They gave money to people who were poor. The kids would qualify, that's for sure. But how could she ask without telling about the kids?

She couldn't.

"Hi, Lassie," said Imogene and Corey. The little boy hugged the collie's neck. Lassie patiently stood while Corey and Imogene fussed over her, stroking her long fur and kissing her damp nose.

"Who takes care of Corey while you go to school?" asked Sarah suddenly.

"He goes to a day-care center near school," said Briny. "Then I pick him up when I get out."

"Who pays for it?" asked Sarah.

Briny shrugged. "I guess it's part of welfare. He's been going there since . . . I mean, when Mom used to work."

"How long until your mom is well?" Sarah asked.

All the kids suddenly stuffed their mouths with bologna or cheese. Sarah looked from one child to the other. Each face was still, eyes cast down. Lassie whined and pushed Sarah's arm with her muzzle.

"What did I say?" asked Sarah, a little bugged.

Briny raised her gaze and met Sarah's eyes coolly.

"What would you say if we told you our mother was dead?"

Sarah's eyes widened. "Dead?" She hadn't expected that.

Briny chewed on the end of a strand of her red hair. "Mom died exactly five weeks ago today," she said calmly. "We stayed in the apartment until the first of the month, then we had to leave because we didn't have rent."

"We had to leave our toys and stuff," said Gus.

"I had to leave Mr. Green Bear," said Corey solemnly. "I miss him. But I miss Mom more."

"Cal tried to pick up the welfare check," Gabby took over the explaining. "But they wouldn't let a kid sign for it. So no money for us."

"Didn't anyone wonder where you'd go after your mom died?" asked Sarah.

"Sure," said Briny. "We told the social worker we were going to live with our grandparents in Des Moines. Cal and I called the social worker the next day and gave her all the information she wanted. We pretended to be old, disguised our voices, you know. Faked her out good. Then we took the kids and hid wherever we could. We didn't know where to go," she continued. "We knew if we went to a shelter or something they'd throw us into foster care."

"We would never see each other again," said Gabby.

"We slept in the park for two nights, in bushes. Then we found this place," said Briny. "It seemed perfect. And when we went back to school, we told our teachers that our grandparents decided to move here so that we wouldn't have any more trauma in our lives."

"How about your dad?" asked Sarah. "Can't you stay with him?"

"Which one?" asked Gabby sarcastically.

"What do you mean?" Sarah asked. How could they have more than one father?

"She means," explained Briny, a fire in her eyes, "that we have different fathers. Cal and I have the same father, but Gabby and Angus each have a different father. Imogene and Corey have the same father."

Sarah's head spun. "Do you know where any of your fathers are?" How weird it sounded. Fathers. Not really a stepfather, just a bunch of fathers.

Briny shrugged. She gave Lassie the last piece of her cheese. "My father is in the state prison," she said.

"Prison!" That seemed worse than death. "Why?"

"Because he's stupid. He got caught selling drugs."

Sarah couldn't imagine talking about her father like that, not to mention she couldn't imagine Dad selling drugs.

A silence fell over the group.

Finally, Sarah spoke, "I can hardly believe your story. It seems like something I heard on the six o'clock news or a made-up TV story."

"What's strange is that everybody bought the story and just sort of forgot about us," Briny said. "I guess we're one of those families that fell through the cracks in the system."

Looking around the barn, Sarah tried to sort out their present life. She had seen some blankets—a couple were ancient horse blankets from the barn. They each had some clothes. A few pots in which Briny cooked simple stuff over a fire. But how did they wash themselves, their clothes—actually not much washing went on as she had smelled, but what about everything else? What if one of them got sick? Little kids got sick a lot.

Briny seemed to be on Sarah's wave length. She waved her hand toward the back of the barn. "We picked this place because it's vacant. But the well still works if you really pump hard. It's one of those old-fashioned kind, so you don't need electricity. We can wash up there and wash our clothes and hang them over the stall dividers."

"Isn't it cold water?"

Briny shrugged. "Yeah."

"It's really cold," said Imogene. "Briny makes me stick my head under it so she can wash my hair."

"She always cries," said Gus.

"My hair is longer than yours!" yelled Imogene. "That's why."

"The food I don't bring?" asked Sarah.

Briny shrugged again. "I told you. I have my ways."

"She takes it," said Gabby.

Sarah, again, was shocked.

"What would you do?" asked Briny, sternly.

What would she do? She just couldn't imagine herself alone like that. "Don't you have grandparents?" she began when Gabby gave a snort.

"Sure we do. They could care less about us," she said.

"Only Mama cared about us," said Gus.

Corey's eyes filled up. "I want Mama!" He began crying.

Briny scooped him up. "I swipe the food, okay? Cop it. Shoplift it," said Briny impatiently. "Do I need to draw a picture?" She bounced Corey on her hip. He stopped crying, but dirty streaks lined his cheeks.

"Steal it?" Sarah couldn't keep her voice from rising.

"You want us to starve?" asked Briny. She pulled Imogene close, wiped her running nose with her sleeve, all with one arm. "You want this little kid to go hungry?"

"No, of course not," Sarah said sadly. But stealing food. But what was Sarah doing? Taking money and food from her parents? *Isn't it mine, too?* She thought, *I'm a member of the family, I should be able to give away some food and money if I want.*

Since her jewelry box was empty and her parents would get suspicious if any more money vanished from the vase, Sarah swallowed hard and asked Briny, "So how do you do it?"

Briny cocked her head. "What?"

"You know, take stuff."

The Shoppers

That night Jimmy and Katie made more phone calls. They'd been directing the donors to send the checks to the church address, rather than home. Dad had said, "It sounds more professional."

They had attached a longer phone line to Dad's phone and had dragged it partway down the stairs so Katie could sit halfway up and peer over the banister at Jimmy on the phone in the kitchen. She waved at him.

"We need a wireless phone," Jimmy muttered.

"Dream on," Mom told him from the kitchen table where she working on the accounts for the unwed mothers' house. Mom was a whiz in math. She helped Jimmy with his prealgebra when he got stuck.

"We have a new computer at the store. It has a modem with an answering machine, fax, and speaker phone," said Katie. "It's cool."

"Yeah, Mom," said Jimmy. "It's cool. So why don't we live in the present and get a cordless phone like most people have had for twenty years?"

"Dream on," said Mom again.

Sarah came downstairs, stepping carefully around Katie, the phone, her papers, and wandered into the kitchen. She filled a glass with water.

"Quiet," hissed Jimmy. "I'm on the phone."

"You're always on the phone," said Sarah in a not-so-quiet voice. He glared at her. She stared back as she drank the entire glass of water. She turned on the water, full blast, and filled the glass a second time.

Jimmy, in the middle of talking to a donor, scowled hard at her. She dumped the half-full glass into the sink. The water splashed. He shook his fist at her and drew a forefinger across his throat, then pointed at her. She turned her back on her brother and stalked upstairs, taking exaggerated care to step around Katie who was totally in the way.

As Sarah walked into her room, the idea hit her. She would take the collie bank with all the money collected for fund raising. Some of the money was in check form, which she couldn't use, but a lot of it was cash.

She'd take it on Sunday. That was a good day because kids had been selling tickets all weekend. Jimmy collected the money after school on Friday and Dad wouldn't deposit it until Monday.

Sarah lay in bed that night, imagining herself taking

Jimmy's bank. She still felt bad about stealing. After all, stealing was totally wrong. God wrote not to steal in stone when He wrote the Ten Commandments. What could she do? She couldn't let the kids go hungry. Besides, weren't the Freedmans more important than a stupid rodeo?

Saturday morning Sarah had to help with laundry, mop the kitchen floor, vacuum all downstairs, and do the breakfast dishes. She felt as if she were a chambermaid! No one else she knew had to do as many chores as she did.

Finally when she was done, she said, "I'm going over to Monique's, okay?" Monique had bragged about going to Dubuque for the weekend, so Sarah knew if Mom got it in her head to phone she'd just get the Garcias' answering machine.

Sarah slipped on her backpack. It was light for once— she had packed only a roll of toilet paper and paper towels. Sarah and Lassie walked as if going to Monique's, in case Mom should step outside to check the mail. Then when they were down the street and out of sight, she and Lassie doubled back to the outskirts of town.

Near the farm, Lassie romped ahead and darted into the barn first. Sarah smiled at the laughter and shouts of "Lassie! Lassie!" as if her dog were a celebrity.

When Sarah walked into the dimness, Briny, who was up in the hayloft, called, "Ready?"

Sarah swallowed hard. "Today?" she asked with reservation.

"Today," said Briny.

Sarah took out the paper goodies and set them on the rickety, goat-milking stand. "Okay," she agreed.

For the first time since Sarah had been at the barn, Cal was there too, his hair tousled. He climbed down from the hayloft. Shadows fell over his face, and he looked older as if he were a grown-up.

"Hi, Cal," Sarah said.

He wiggled his fingers at her and walked out of the barn. Boys! He was as bad as Jimmy. Briny scrambled down the ladder, a worn backpack slung over her shoulder.

Lassie loped up and down the length of the barn, her mouth open, tongue lolling like a pink tie. Gus, Corey, and Imogene ran after the big dog. When Lassie halted, Imogene fearlessly flung her arms around the collie and kissed her nose.

Imogene declared, "I love you, Lassie!"

"Guess she's over her fear of dogs," said Sarah.

"At least with Lassie. Now if she wouldn't be so scared of grown-ups," said Briny adjusting her pack straps.

"What does she do in school?" asked Sarah.

"Live in fear," said Briny darkly. "She's scared that some grown-up will take her away from us."

Sarah glanced at the five year old gaily chatting to

Lassie and wished she could do more. But what?

A little voice said, *Tell Dad*. But she couldn't, could she? She had promised, and besides, could Dad do anything?

"We'll be back in a couple of hours," Briny called. "Tell Cal, okay?" Gabby nodded.

Sarah told Lassie, "Stay here, girl. Stay with Imogene and the kids."

Sarah and Briny peered outside carefully, then hurried to the front of the barn to the road where they wouldn't be trespassing if seen, and then headed for the shopping strip.

"It's easy to do," said Briny. "But you have to be careful. Most stores have a video camera. Just be sure your back is to it. It helps to have two people working together."

Working together. She was a ten-year-old partner-in-crime. It gave her heart a heavy feeling. She wasn't cut out for this. It made her feel sick to her stomach.

As they got closer to the shopping strip, Sarah's heart pounded more than when she'd had to talk in front of church last year, telling how God helped her. She thought grimly, *Wouldn't the church members be shocked if they knew?* But if they knew, would they help the kids find a place to live and food? Maybe.

The youth pastor, Pastor Sam, would help. Sarah thought about him as they walked the last street to the stores. Briny chattered about different things she wanted to "buy." She always said jokingly, "Stuff we're going to buy."

Sarah brooded over whether she should tell Pastor Sam. If anyone would understand the kids, he probably would. Maybe she could write him a letter and not sign her name.

Briny nudged her. "Are you listening?"

Sarah focused on her. "What?"

Briny rolled her eyes. "I said, which store do you want to hit first?"

Hit. Sounded like a bank robbery. "I don't care," she said, uneasy they had arrived so fast. She wished they could just keep walking and never get there.

Briny studied the stores a minute. "There's a sale over at Wooden's Drug Store. That might be good because it looks crowded," said Briny. "Did you bring some cash?"

Sarah handed her two dollars. She had four dollars total. Briny had asked her to bring a little money, which Sarah didn't have. So she had explored the depths of Dad's wallet, hoping he didn't count his change too often.

"Okay," said Briny. "Just relax. Pretend we're just looking, having fun."

Sarah took a deep breath. Fear spiked against her like a scratchy wool shirt.

They walked into Wooden's Drug Store, Briny swinging her back pack by the handles like a happy-go-lucky kid. Sarah pasted a fake smile on her face and desperately wished she could at least pray, but you couldn't pray to successfully steal, could you?

Chaos Within

Inside Wooden's Drug Store, people strolled and children trotted the aisles. Shopping carts jammed the clearance and the toy aisles.

Sarah and Briny first walked casually along the makeup aisle. At least Briny did. Sarah's legs moved as if in deep sand, stiff and awkward.

"Look at this," said Briny. She picked up a ponytail holder made with gold threads and metallic green ribbon. "Lean down like you're looking at stuff on the counter there," Briny commanded in a whisper.

Sarah did, her heart pounding so hard that it hurt. She forced herself to pick up some bath oil beads shaped like stars and shells that she never would look at normally.

Briny unzipped the top of Sarah's backpack and something small dropped in. Sarah held her breath, squeezing a bath oil bead until she was afraid the scallop shell would pop.

Briny strolled on down the aisle. "Look at these earrings," she called gaily. Sarah, like a tin soldier, slowly rose and followed her friend. The small weight in her pack seemed heavier than an army of tin soldiers.

⚜

Imogene peeked outside the barn. No one was around. Corey was napping upstairs in the trapdoor room, the door propped open. Gus was playing with his birthday toys, creating little corrals and forts out of sticks and bits of wood. Gabby and Cal were playing a card game. So she called softly to Lassie and they scurried across the barnyard, dodging bushes of yellow flowers, upright and certain they belonged there.

"I wish we belonged somewhere," said Imogene softly. Lassie whined and nuzzled the little girl. Together they crossed into a thicket of vines growing wild over and across an old wire clotheslines. Imogene had to duck to creep inside the vine cave. In there she felt safer. Cal said that soon berries would ripen and they could eat as much as they wanted. Imogene would like to sit in the safe place and eat juicy, ripe berries.

After they crept along the narrow path, Imogene and Lassie followed another faint trail that led to the pond. The pond was also a safe place, and Imogene named the pond and her small woods "Lassie's Laughing Place."

Sarah had told her that when Lassie opened her mouth and put out her tongue, teeth showing, she was laughing

91

in a dog way. Lassie did that a lot at the pond. So, of course, it was "Lassie's Laughing Place."

Imogene yanked off her faded green and blue striped tennis shoes. They were a little small for her, and her toes wanted out.

She waded into the still, green water. The mud was gooshy and cold. But the sun was bright and warmed up the air. Among the weeping willows around the pond, the filtered light turned a soft golden green.

Lassie lay on the bank, nose on her forelegs, watching the little girl splash about. Imogene was picking watercress for a salad. Cal had brought some limp carrots and cucumbers from the big trash bin in back of the nearest grocery store.

Imogene lifted her shirt into a pouch and lay the round watercress leaves like a bouquet in her shirt. Lassie growled, low, deep.

"What, girl?" Imogene asked as she'd heard Sarah question the collie. The dog stood up and the fur along her back also stood up in a long ridge along her spine. Lassie stared back the way they had come, her lips pulled into a snarl.

Imogene stepped out of the water, still clutching the watercress, when Lassie suddenly slipped away into the small forest of cattails at the far end of the pond.

Imogene started to follow when a deep, big voice said, "Stay where you are, little girl."

Sarah wanted to crawl under Wooden's display counter and hide. Her guts twisted. "I've got to go to the bathroom," she hissed.

"Now?" asked Briny, leaning over the bargain table.

"Now," said Sarah desperately.

"Give me your backpack," said Briny. Sarah handed it over and ran for the bathroom, back in the stockroom.

After she'd used the toilet, she stood washing her hands and staring at her reflection in the old mirror. Some of the silver on the back had come off, and all the reflections seemed dirty and spider webbed. Sarah reluctantly returned to Briny.

Briny thrust her pack at Sarah, her eyes dancing. The pack was definitely heavier. "What's in here?" whispered Sarah. Briny grabbed her arm and dragged her back down the aisle with toys. Briny neatly lifted two plastic bags of jewel-colored marbles, leaned close to Sarah, and slipped one into her jeans' front pocket. The other she held up as if showing Sarah, then hung back on the peg.

"Just some stuff," she said smugly. Sarah slipped on the pack, her heart heavy with fear and guilt.

"I thought you were going to get some food," whispered Sarah.

"We are," said Briny, "but the kids need some other stuff, too. Like shampoo."

"Is that what's in here?"

"Yeah," said Briny as she dragged Sarah down the food aisle. "Look, I'm going to do something to cause a bit of commotion. When I do you grab a couple boxes of granola bars, okay? Maybe some crackers, too?"

"I don't know. The boxes are kind of big. What if someone sees me?"

Briny sighed impatiently. "Do you want to do the distracting then?"

"Like what?" she asked when someone called, "Hello, Sarah Harmon."

Sarah nearly collapsed. Mrs. Huntz with frizzy gray hair from church strode toward them.

"Act normal," hissed Briny. "Quit looking like a caught mouse."

Sarah fixed a smile on her face and said, "Hi, Mrs. Huntz. How are you today?" To her ears, her voice sounded like someone had run it through one of the sound changers and stretched it out like a rubber band.

But Mrs. Huntz, the major motor mouth that she was, didn't seem to notice. She just launched in. "Well, Sarah, I've been having such problems with my arthritis. You have no idea. My fingers are knotted up—"

Knotted up like my guts, thought Sarah, standing first on one leg, then on the other leg, trying to listen. But her thoughts kept parading through her skull, crowding out Mrs. Huntz's words.

Briny brushed by Sarah, whispering, "One distraction coming up. Remember what to get."

Sarah really clammed up. She only nodded at Mrs. Huntz, having absolutely no idea what the older woman was saying. Of course, Mrs. Huntz hardly needed responses. She mostly wanted a warm body to yack at. The woman talked on, waving her hand encrusted with a ring on almost every finger. At one point Sarah said nervously, "Maybe that's why your fingers hurt."

Mrs Huntz stopped. "What, dear?"

"All your rings. Aren't they heavy on your fingers? Maybe they make your fingers hurt."

"For goodness sake," sputtered Mrs. Huntz. "What a perfectly ridiculous thing to say."

Sarah's face burned red with shame. Before she could put her foot in her mouth any farther, a big crash erupted in the next aisle over. The older woman turned, never at a loss for words, and called, "Anyone hurt? What fell? Can I help?"

Sarah simply fled.

For a moment the store went quiet except for Mrs. Huntz's yammer and the awful instrumental version of an old Beatles tune. A couple of smaller crashes echoed after the first, then people erupted in yells and talk and exclamations that drowned out Mrs. Huntz and the awful Beatles remake. Sarah half-ran down the food aisle, snatched up two boxes of granola bars and a box of whole wheat crackers. She stuck them under one arm, headed for the door, then stood by the checkout uncertain what to do. Cashiers and customers paid no attention to her. Their eyes were fixed on the chaos.

A loudspeaker called all the stock boys to aisle five. Sarah heard one of the cashiers say a big cosmetic display had fallen over.

A customer said that she saw a shopping cart hit the edge of the display. "Must have hit hard," commented the cashier.

Sarah bet it did.

Briny materialized at her side. "Ready to blow this joint?" she asked, giggling. Sarah wanted to disappear.

Briny took the granola bars and crackers. She walked up to one of the chatty cashiers. "We didn't get a bag for our purchase. Can we have one?"

The cashier barely glanced at her. "Sure, hon," and handed her a paper bag that read "Wooden Drug Store, since 1964." Briny put the boxes in the paper bag and the girls walked out.

"What a madhouse," said Briny.

But Sarah carried the chaos in her heart.

No Safe Place

Imogene froze. Her legs wouldn't obey her brain, which screamed, *Run!* Fear paralyzed her body.

The man was as big as a ship and pushed through the weeping willow branches. His uniform told Imogene that he was the sheriff.

He shoved through the last curtain of branches. Imogene's knees gave out and she sank down, her watercress spilling over her knees.

"Little girl," the man said again, his voice kindly. "I won't hurt you. I'm Sheriff Johnson. I just want to ask you a couple of questions."

Imogene stared up at him, stricken.

"Do you live around here?" he asked.

She hugged her knees to her chest and stared hard at a hole in the ground. Maybe if she concentrated hard she'd shrink enough to slid into it. A wash of fear broke over her. No, she couldn't do that. She was caught.

He crunched on stalks of cattails. Imogene cowered,

peeping up through her fringe of hair. All she could think was, *Lassie, oh, Lassie!*

"Little girl," the sheriff began again when, like magic, Lassie appeared behind the sheriff. She barked, her teeth gleaming, like a wild creature. Her lovely ruff stood on end, huge. Imogene couldn't make herself small, but Lassie could make herself enormous. The sheriff whirled.

Lassie lunged closer, barking in a nonstop stream. The sheriff yanked free his heavy, long flashlight from his belt. "Easy, girl. Lassie, isn't it?" he said. But Lassie would have no calming. She lunged closer. He swung the flashlight. Lassie dodged, then plunged in again.

Imogene found herself on her feet. A small pleasure shivered through the child for a moment. Lassie came! She came!

As the sheriff turned his back to Imogene, she fled. The pool and its golden-green light unraveled behind her. Lassie's Laughing Place wasn't safe anymore.

In the distance Lassie's fierce barking touched her like a friend's thrown kiss and she ran farther.

On the edge of the farm she shimmied up a tree. When Lassie stopped barking a couple minutes later, Imogene was nearly as high up as the barn hayloft.

She held her breath, waiting. Sure enough the sheriff pushed out of the green arms of willows. He carefully searched all around him. Imogene squeezed her eyes shut. Couldn't she, this once, become a little bug on a leaf?

Below her, bushes rattled like someone crumpling a piece of paper. The sheriff was coming closer! She pushed her face against the rough bark of the thick branch, her eyes still closed. *Go away, go away,* she chanted silently.

More rustling. Then silence. A gentle silence that coaxed her to open her eyes. When she looked down, Lassie sat alone, under the tree, her large, chocolate-colored eyes staring up. The sheriff was gone.

"Oh, Lassie," Imogene whispered. "You saved me." She wept a few tears of relief as she climbed down the tree. She scraped her elbow on a ragged branch and cried a little more. When she stopped, she dried her tears on Lassie's fur. The dog walked her back to Cal and Gabby.

"Imogene!" Gabby gasped. "The sheriff—"

"I'm okay," said Imogene. "Lassie watched over me."

When Sarah and Briny return from their shopping, they climbed up the ladder. Sarah dumped out her backpack. Little bottles of three different kinds of shampoo, a tube of toothpaste, the glittery ponytail holder, a box of neon markers, two small pads of paper and a bottle of soap bubbles all fell out onto the loft's floor.

Cal was also up in the hayloft. He put down a textbook and stared at Briny. Sarah could see a family storm coming and she just wanted to go home. She started to get up when Cal said in such a tight, angry voice that she sat afraid, rooted to the floor. "Did you take this stuff, Briny?"

Briny tossed her hair and snapped her gum. "What do you think?"

"I told you to knock that off."

"Fine," she said. "When you come up with the cash to buy stuff I'll be more than happy to stop."

Cal's lips tightened. His eyes deepened. Sarah wanted to crawl under the trapdoor.

Briny, seemingly not noticing her brother's rage, pulled out stuff from her backpack and spread it out on the floor. Then she opened the paper bag and said, "The cashier actually gave us the bag to put our stuff in. Don't worry, Cal. Sarah and I were careful."

Cal glanced at Sarah as if he'd just noticed her. "You're Jim Harmon's sister, aren't you?"

Sarah nodded as Briny blew a big, pink bubble. Cal pointed at Sarah. "This kid is going to get you in major trouble. Her dad is a pastor."

"So." Briny's bubble popped. She picked the gum off her lips and the end of her nose.

"So, if she gets caught shoplifting, everyone will know about us," said Cal.

"I'd never tell," said Sarah quickly. "Really. They could torture me and I wouldn't tell."

Briny lifted her hand to Sarah as if to say, "See?" Briny added, "Besides, I don't get caught. I'll see that she doesn't either."

Cal sighed impatiently and held up a plastic bead necklace. "This is hardly something we need."

Briny snatched it from him. "The kids need toys, Cal. We have nothing, okay? That store can spare some stuff. Quit frothing at the mouth. You'll give yourself ulcers."

Cal threw down his book and stomped down the ladder. Lassie whined downstairs.

"I'd better go," Sarah told Briny. "Tomorrow I don't think I'll get here. Sunday school, church, and all." She had thought about inviting the kids to go, but couldn't bring herself to ask them. It was too weird. Shoplifting with Briny, then going to church?

Besides, what if Mrs. Huntz said something to Mom about Sarah and Briny being at the store? No, the risk was too great.

Sarah and Lassie walked home in the lingering ribbons of light. Last year when she had the flu for three weeks, it was as if she would never get over being queasy and tired. She had just wanted to pull the covers over her head and go to sleep. That's what she wanted to do now.

But this time she wouldn't get better. She'd be getting worse because tomorrow she had to take the collie bank from Jimmy's room. Things were getting out of hand. How did she get so tangled up in this? All she ever wanted to do was help a family of kids who were hungry and cold!

The Collie Bank Crime

Luke Castillo is coming to my birthday party," Monique whispered to Sarah during the church service.

Sarah looked sideways at Monique. She had a way of getting under your skin.

"I already know what present he's going to get me," Monique continued. Sitting strategically behind Sarah, Mom cleared her throat. The first warning. But Sarah had to know about Luke.

The last refrain of the song began, and Sarah leaned over to Monique. "How do you know what he's getting you?"

"I saw him at Donnelley's in Dubuque." The Harmons never shopped at Donnelley's—it was out of their league.

Monique tossed her permed hair. "He was looking at a necklace with a real diamond in it, and when he saw me, he tried to hide it. I couldn't go talk to him because I was with my mom. But he smiled at me and hid the necklace behind his back."

Life is not fair, Sarah thought. Maybe Monique was just making that up. Either way, Sarah wanted to kick Monique. That wasn't a very Christian attitude, but she wasn't exactly racking up points in that category, anyhow.

The song ended and everyone sat down, almost time for kids to leave to go down to Sunday school. Sarah longed to get away from Monique.

Monique giggled into her hands and whispered, "At lunch Friday I told Luke that you thought he was cute."

"Monique!" Sarah's voice skyrocketed to the church rafters. One woman in the row in front of the girls turned around and frowned at them.

Mom's finger came down hard on Sarah's shoulder. Sarah jumped. "Sarah Elizabeth Harmon," Mom whispered loudly. Sarah's face burned.

After a prayer, Dad said that all the children were excused to go to their Sunday school classes. As Sarah and Monique stood to file out, Monique said, "Your middle name is Elizabeth? That sounds so weird." Sarah thought Monique was getting weird.

In the hallway, they caught up with Jessica and Kristin, and Monique repeated Sarah's middle name. "Isn't her middle name corny?" she mocked. Kristin and Jessica laughed in a mean way.

Sarah's face burned again, and she decided they weren't her friends anymore.

The date: Sunday afternoon. The time: 3:34 P.M. The place: Jimmy's room. The crime: the robbery of the collie bank.

Sarah was terrified. Her stomach ached. She desperately wanted to pray. What could she say? God, please don't let anyone see me stealing the donated money from KidsTown. Yeah, right.

Sarah slipped outside her bedroom door and stood in the hall. She chewed on her lower lip. No one else was upstairs. Dad was visiting ancient Mrs. Miller who had broken her hip last week. Mom was in the kitchen fixing dinner. Jimmy and his stupid ticket sellers, Katie, Blake, and Briny's weird brother, Cal, were downstairs discussing the rodeo that would begin in six days.

All clear.

Sarah took a deep breath. She held it, wishing she could just float away like a soap bubble. Then silently she snuck down the hall past the bathroom, to her brother's room. His door was half open. She peeked in. His bed was sloppily made. Rumpled dirty clothes littered the floor. Papers were strewn all over his roll-top desk.

She was jealous of that desk. She had wanted it when Grandma Harmon had moved from her rambling farmhouse in eastern Iowa to a retirement home closer to Farley. But Jimmy, as the oldest, had gotten it.

She stuck her tongue out at the photo of Jimmy and

Lassie winning a ribbon in a dog obedience class at the fair. *He always gets the best of everything,* she thought miserably.

She went to the desk and laid her hands on the smooth wood. The roll-top was pushed up, exposing all the little and big compartments. No collie bank in there. She pulled open the four desk drawers and found only paper and stuff.

Where did he keep it? She had seen the bank last week on his bookshelf. His three untidy shelves of books, rocks, fossils, and arrowheads didn't hold a collie bank.

His closet?

She opened the door. The hinges squeaked. She gasped and froze, midstep. Voices drifted upstairs, unchanged. So Sarah pulled the string turning on the closet light. More dirty clothes were spilled over Jimmy's shoes. She kicked through them. No ceramic collie.

Could he have the bank downstairs? He'd entered all the cash and checks yesterday after the mail had come, and had sat at the kitchen table counting and recounting the school money.

Unless he had put it in one of the many boxes up on the top shelf, it wasn't in his closet.

She turned off the light and shut the closet door when footsteps struck the wooden stairs. She wheeled around. Where to hide? She squeezed between the bedroom door and the wall. She would be hidden unless someone came into Jimmy's room.

"Please don't let them find me. Please, please," she prayed, even though she knew God wouldn't honor such a prayer.

Someone climbed to the top of the stairs. Through the crack between the door and the doorsill, she saw Cal Freedman walk past Jimmy's room. She heard his shoes click on the bathroom floor.

Of course. The downstairs bathroom toilet wasn't working too well.

She waited until Cal went back downstairs. Hours seemed to go by. Sarah's legs ached from standing in one place. Finally, Cal walked back down the hall and clumped downstairs.

Now where would Jimmy keep that bank?

She looked under his pillow, in his underwear drawer, behind the dresser. Then she dropped to her hands and knees. Sarah lifted the edge of the hanging bedspread, one with a print of football players running, catching balls, tackling each other, all for a dumb ball.

She poked her head under the bed. Next to a couple of dust balls, an old soda can, and a library book about football, lay the collie bank.

Motive Madness

Before she dashed back to her room, Sarah slid open Jimmy's bedroom window. Then she unlatched the screen and pushed. The plastic mesh fell the two stories, landing on top of one of Mom's rose bushes.

Then she turned, the bank clasped against her chest. Lassie stood in the doorway.

The dog stared mournfully at her, brown eyes sad, ears drooping.

"Go away," Sarah hissed, hardly able to believe what she was saying. "Go away, Lassie. Just go away."

But Lassie didn't move. She seemed as a dog carved out of stone, sad and accusing. Sarah fled around her and dove into her own room where she firmly shut the door.

That night after Sarah had gone to bed, she waited for what she knew would come. She didn't know when, . . . but she knew it would happen.

Sometime later, Jimmy hollered, "My bank is gone!"

Sarah threw her covers over her head. If only the warm

darkness would protect her forever. But under her cheerful, red and purple flannel nightgown, which curled around her bare legs, lay a certain ceramic lump.

Dad and Mom were in their room, the radio playing oldies, when Jimmy burst down the hall. Lassie, like a kite tail, galloped behind.

Jimmy skidded into his parents' room. "The ticket money's gone," he bawled like a lost calf.

"Are you sure, son?" Dad, Jimmy, and Lassie milled outside Sarah's partially open door.

Jimmy was half undressed, his shirt off, jeans still on. "My window's open and the screen's outside," Jimmy told Dad. "Someone stole the ticket money. The whole bank is gone."

"Let me see," said Dad, ever calm. Sarah could shut her eyes and see them clearly in Jimmy's room, searching.

Mom appeared in her doorway. "Are you awake, Sarah?" she whispered.

"Yes," Sarah answered softly.

Mom sat on the edge of her bed. Sarah stiffened, moving her legs to cover the bank.

"I'm scared," said Sarah truthfully.

Mom stroked her hair. "It's okay, honey."

No, it's not, thought Sarah. *If you only knew, you wouldn't be so kind to me.*

Dad poked his head in the doorway. "I'll call the sheriff."

The sheriff!

At school during lunch on Monday, the Wacky Rodeo committee discussed what had happened. Katie and Jimmy were sitting on the bench in the middle of the school center. On the narrow patch of grass across from the bench, Blake lay on his side.

Katie turned to Jimmy. "Do you want to know what I think?"

"What if I said no?" he teased.

Katie ploughed on anyway, "I really think that Cal took the money."

"Katie!" Jimmy and Blake hollered.

"Think about it, guys. He was upstairs supposedly in the bathroom, alone."

"So were you," said Blake.

"I don't have a motive to steal the money," she said.

"And Cal does?"

"Think about it," said Katie.

"I *am* thinking about it," snapped Jimmy.

"Didn't the sheriff totally rule out a burglar coming in the window?" asked Blake. He sat up, pushing his glasses farther up the bridge of his nose.

"He said someone coming in the window would push the screen into the house. The screen was outside. And the screen latches from the inside," Jimmy added.

"You're sure the bank was under your bed?" asked Blake.

Jimmy nodded wearily. "Besides, Dad and I ripped my

room apart, looking, just in case. Nothing."

"When did you have it last?" asked Katie.

"It was Saturday evening because I was still double-checking the amounts."

Blake took off his glasses and twirled them.

"Did the sheriff go to Cal's house?" asked Katie.

"Katie!" She had a one-track mind.

"He's a suspect," she said stubbornly.

"We all are," said Blake.

She stuck out her tongue at him. "So let the sheriff come talk to us. I don't have anything to hide. Is he going to Cal's?"

Jimmy sighed. "What have you got against Cal?"

"I don't trust him," she said and tossed her empty milk carton into the nearby trash can. "And you shouldn't either."

"How can you say that?" asked Blake. "You don't even know the guy."

"He was in my biology class last fall. He wasn't my partner, that's true, but he was Lindsey's. She told me that he told her that his family was really poor, that they used food stamps and were on welfare and stuff because his mom was sick. I don't know, cancer or something. Anyway, he dropped the class after a few weeks."

"Has it occurred to you that maybe he needs a friend?" Jimmy asked. He didn't think he'd been much of a friend himself. He hardly talked to the guy.

Katie gave him a long look. "He needs money. That's obvious. So why all of a sudden is he getting on school committees? And he gets on a committee that deals with money. How convenient."

"The teacher did appoint him," Jimmy reminded her. Katie only shrugged.

"She has a point," said Blake. "I hate to make him guilty before we know. But it does sound suspicious."

"You guys watch too much TV," said Jimmy, but a grim reality was sinking in his gut.

Blake twirled his glasses some more. "Maybe we should talk to him."

"How are we going to do that?" asked Jimmy. "What if he didn't do it? It would be awful to blame him."

"Leave it to me," said Katie.

"Where angels fear to tread," said Blake.

Jimmy finished the quote in his head: *fools rush in*. He knew Katie thought of it too, because she turned red, but whether from shame or anger, he wasn't sure.

"I don't know, Katie," said Jimmy. "I'm not sure talking to him is a good idea."

The warning bell jangled. Lunch was over. Jimmy wished this whole thing was over. He wasn't sure meeting Blair Coughlin was worth all this.

Guilty without a Trial

Monday afternoon Sarah warily approached the old barn. Jimmy had taken Lassie with him to Katie's house. Her backpack was heavy with the collie bank, the checks, and the cash. The cash! Over one hundred and forty dollars! She tried to imagine Briny's face when she handed over the money. That would keep the kids in food for, how long? Weeks?

But then what? Where would she get money next? She didn't want to think about that.

She pushed open the barn door.

After school Jimmy, Katie, and Blake walked to Jimmy's house to get Lassie so she could play with Katie's dog, Rags. Then they went up into the playroom over the garage.

"What are we going to do?" asked Jimmy. He sat on the floor, his knees drawn up, his chin resting on his knee caps.

Katie perched on the edge of the long table in the center of the room, kicking her heels against the table leg. A jumble of electric train tracks, halves of mountains, and other miniatures lay on the table. With each thump of her heels she punctuated her words. "We need a way . . ." *thump* ". . . to earn back . . ." *thump* ". . . the money that was . . ." *thump!* ". . . stolen."

"Maybe Cal should be responsible for that," said Blake from the saggy couch.

"So you think he took the money too?" Jimmy asked.

Katie rolled her eyes. "Look, Jim, what is the zip code for the state of denial? The whole school thinks he did it," she said sarcastically.

"I just don't know," said Jimmy. He was getting a headache. "I guess I don't want to believe he did it."

During lunch, a bunch of kids had gathered around Jimmy, all talking about the theft. They didn't have to say one word about Cal, except he had been there.

"I bet that Cal did it," said one kid darkly. The words took flight and soon every kid in eighth grade knew that Cal Freedman had stolen the ticket money.

"Why did he cut school then?" asked Katie. "Lindsey and I both saw him this morning. He was kind of skulking around the downstairs boys' bathroom."

When Jimmy got home, Mom told him that the sheriff had called and said that Cal Freedman's address on his school records was wrong. No Freeman family lived there.

"I just knew it," Katie had muttered after hearing that.

Jimmy sighed. "Back to what are we going to do about the stolen money?" The cash was gone, vanished forever. The checks could be rewritten. The school office and KidsTown were figuring out how to let the donors who had written checks know, so they could cancel the stolen checks, then write new ones.

Blake said, "Call them and explain what happened?"

Jimmy shook his head. "They'd probably think I was just a careless kid and why should they give me more money?" The only thing Jimmy could think of was something Dad said. "A man has to make his way in this world by working."

Working.

"A bake sale?" suggested Katie doubtfully.

Blake flopped back in the couch. "Maybe set up a ticket table outside one of the stores?"

"I think half of Farley has bought a ticket already," said Katie.

"Maybe we could go to another town?" suggested Blake.

"I know," said Jimmy lifting his head. "We could offer ourselves to do work. Maybe take I.O.U.'s now so we earn back the stolen money. If we charge four dollars an hour, we can earn back the $148 in thirty-seven hours."

"Thirty-seven hours!" screeched Katie. "We'll be working until summer."

"Not with all three of us," said Blake. "That's about thirteen hours each."

"I bet some of the people at church would let us work for them," said Jimmy.

"That's not a bad idea," said Blake. "We could ask some of the other eighth graders to help."

"What about me?" said Katie. "I'm already slaving for Gran."

Jimmy said with a wicked gleam in his eye, "Maybe you could donate some of your paycheck."

For once Katie didn't have anything to say. She finally said in a little voice, "That's probably the right thing to do, isn't it?"

Sarah wondered where the kids were. The barn was empty as if no one lived there at all. There were no kids playing, just silent dust motes drifting down to the dirty wooden floor.

Even though she wasn't in Jimmy's school, Sarah had heard the news that Cal Freedman was being blamed for the stolen money and that he had vanished after his morning classes.

She felt sick to her stomach. Maybe she could just throw the collie bank somewhere and hope it would be found eventually. But Cal being blamed . . . she had never thought that would happen. She figured that some nameless, faceless robber would be blamed.

Maybe what she should do was put the collie bank with

the checks somewhere in the barn, and let someone else find it a long time from now—when things had blown over and the Freedmans had moved to another place. No one goes out to the old barn. No one would think to look there. Then she could just give Briny the cash and say it was from Sarah's savings account. That was it. She'd do that.

She walked lightly in the barn looking for just the right spot to hide the ceramic collie.

Then she thought of the trapdoor. There couldn't be a better place! Sarah climbed the ladder. Quickly she unzipped her backpack, took out all the dollar bills from the bank, stuffed them in her pack, then wiped the bank with her T-shirt. She'd seen a TV show were the crook wiped off fingerprints. *Great,* she thought, *I'm in the league with a crook.* But determinedly she wiped the whole collie's body; then she carefully placed the bank in the secret hiding place and closed the door.

She stepped back, walked around the hayloft. *Good, the bank was hidden.* Then she scrambled back down the ladder and out the barn door. She heard her name being shouted.

Briny and the younger kids were walking toward her along the road. Sarah took a deep breath and met them.

A Tangled Web

At dinner on Tuesday night, Jimmy told his family, "We almost have enough I.O.U.'s for the stolen money."

Sarah winced at the word *stolen*.

Jimmy continued, not noticing, "We're going to do the work after the rodeo because there isn't time this week. A couple of kids from school are going to help too," he went on. "I was thinking after we pay back the stolen money, we might form a club or something, like 'Starving Students, We'll Do Any Job,' and keep working to donate all year to KidsTown."

Dad thoughtfully broke open a biscuit. "Not a bad idea," he said. "I meant to tell you, the church needs the windows washed in the sanctuary."

Jimmy groaned. "Twelve windows!" Big stained-glass scenes of Jesus' life filled two sides of the church walls.

Dad's eyes twinkled. "If you don't want to earn the money—" he began.

"We'll do it," Jimmy said quickly and wrote down something in his notebook. "Four hours with two people working," he muttered and scribbled figures.

Sarah pushed her green beans around on her plate. She should have thought of doing other people's chores to earn money. But she was just one ten year old. Would she have made much for the kids? Not hardly. She shoved the beans into a pile, then unpiled them. She couldn't eat.

"Sarah," began Mom. Sarah jumped. Her fork clattered over her plate and fell to the floor. Lassie walked over and licked it.

Sarah wanted to burst into tears. Nothing was going right.

"You've hardly eaten anything," said Mom. "Are you feeling all right?"

"I'm just not hungry," she said. "Can I be excused?"

"*May* I be excused?" murmured Mom.

Sarah didn't sigh or roll her eyes like she usually did when Mom corrected her grammar. Sarah just patiently asked, "May I be excused?"

"Perhaps she's coming down with something," said Dad. "Didn't I hear that a virus was going around the schools?"

"I'm fine," Sarah said, picking up her Lassie-clean fork.

Mom swirled water in her glass and asked gently, "Something's bothering you, isn't it, Sarah?"

"Sarah's been bothering me for years," said Jimmy.

Sarah ignored them all and merely repeated, "May I be excused?"

Mom looked hard at Sarah. She tried to not flinch under Mom's laser gaze. Finally Mom said, "Take your dishes into the kitchen."

Sarah did and began to climb the stairs.

Jimmy said, "Can I eat her dessert?"

Sarah went into her bedroom before she heard the answer. But she knew it would be yes. Everyone said yes to Jimmy.

Upstairs Sarah tried to read some of her homework— state history. Ick. She flipped through the pages of her text-book, wishing she could send herself back in time, away from all this.

She kept seeing the amazement in Briny's eyes yester-day afternoon when she gave her all that money. Sarah wished she felt happier about giving the money to the kids.

Later that afternoon, the grief in Briny's voice and eyes racked her. Briny told Sarah, "Cal's in trouble. They say he stole money from the ticket sales."

Sarah didn't know what to say. She was trapped any way she went.

Gabby had chimed in saying, "He wouldn't do that. Not Cal."

Sarah sat on the old, goat-milking table, stunned. How stupid she was to not think that Jimmy or his friends would be blamed for the missing money.

Briny had added with a funny, sad smile, "I'm the one whose conscience doesn't bother me much. Cal would rather have needles stuck under his fingernails than steal anything."

"Gross!" Gabby exclaimed.

"But true," said Briny. "Cal's too honest. He hates that I take stuff."

In her room, Sarah closed her book and rolled on her back. She stared up at her ceiling. Two years ago she and Mom had painted the galaxy on the ceiling. The planets. The meteor belt. Then a wild array of stars, blue, red, yellow, even green. Some stars were truly all those colors.

Should she run away? If she did, where could she go? She didn't have any money to take a bus. One set of her grandparents lived in New Mexico. Even if she got there somehow, they'd still call and tell her parents where she was.

Could she live with Briny and the kids? Any other time she probably could have, but Briny would want to know why she was running away. Sarah couldn't tell her it was because she took the ticket money. Somehow she thought Briny would see through any lie she concocted. Oh, the whole thing had gotten so tangled and complicated, she'd never get free of it.

Sarah turned off her light and curled up in a ball under her covers. She half dozed when her bedroom door clicked open. The door slowly widened. Toenails clicked on her hardwood floor, then muffled clicks as they struck the dark blue square rug.

Sarah opened her eyes and leaned over the bed. Lassie, of course. Lassie whined. "Oh, Lassie," she breathed. "What am I going to do?"

The collie jumped onto the bed and laid down beside Sarah. She whined again and nuzzled Sarah's chin.

"I'm sorry I told you to go away," Sarah told her. "You're my only friend these days. I couldn't bear it if you were mad at me too."

A little voice said, *Sarah, you have another friend. He's an understanding friend. He loves you. And oh, Sarah, He grieves over you.*

Sarah wept into Lassie's soft fur, until she fell asleep.

Monster Machines

On Thursday afternoon before the rodeo, Jimmy, Blake, and Katie sat on the back porch of Jimmy's house, facing out toward the farmlands, green, rolling, dotted with thickets of trees.

"So where has he been?" asked Katie. She'd asked that about fifty million times. Jimmy didn't even bother to answer. He was sick of thinking about it. Cal had been missing from school since Monday morning. The sheriff's department was still searching for him and his family. In fact, all the Freedman kids had vanished from school on Tuesday, simply disappeared like the end of a bad virus.

The sheriff had also discovered that the kids were runaways from the state. They should be in foster homes because their mom was dead, not sick. They had no other relatives available to take responsibility for them.

"I'm just saying it's really odd," continued Katie.

"You know what?" said Blake to her.

"What?" she replied.

"I think you need to stop talking about that boy and start praying for him."

"Why? He's a thief. He's a—"

Blake interrupted, "Well, I seem to remember a story about Jesus and a thief."

Katie's face flamed. "Oh."

Jimmy leaned back in Mom's old, wicker rocking chair, just letting his thoughts drift around his head like smoke. Ticket selling, in person and on the phone. The rodeo coming up fast. He'd find out tomorrow if his eighth-grade class sold the most tickets or not. He imagined Blair Coughlin signing his name in a special autograph book Jimmy had bought. Blair (of course, they'd be on a first-name basis) would say, "Why, Jim Harmon. That's a good name for a football player. I'll see you in the pros."

More thoughts drifted across his brain, daydreams, fragile as cobwebs, strong as spider venom. Then the smoke of his dreams fluttered across the sky. He sat upright. The rocker creaked in protest.

No, not smoke exactly. Dust? The wind was hardly blowing. Besides Iowa wasn't exactly the dust bowl or a desert.

"What is that brown cloud?" Jimmy asked.

They all stared. A mound of brownish dust slinked up, shaped like a fast rising muffin.

"Strange," said Katie. "It doesn't look like someone plowing. That doesn't look right."

"It's like something exploded," said Blake.

Jimmy said suddenly, "Sarah and Lassie like to walk that way." The three of them exchanged glances.

"Maybe we ought to go over there," said Blake. "We could hit a couple of farms about the rodeo if nothing's going on."

❦

Sarah and Lassie paused at the edge of the farm boundary. They were heading toward the farm to see if the kids had returned. Suddenly, roaring engine noises rumbled the air. What could that be? Someone was going to plow the old farm's land after all?

Somehow she knew that wasn't it and began to run, Lassie leaping ahead of her in bounds, a gold and silver dart aiming for the old barn.

No, it couldn't be. Sarah gasped, a pain stabbing her side. Bulldozers! Two of them, like the bald- headed turkey buzzards, gathering for a kill, rumbling next to the barn.

She ran harder, her backpack thumping her spine with each jolting stride. Lassie pulled far ahead and slowed as she came to the old, rotting spilt-rail fence halfway around the well. Then the collie shot around the corner of the barn and Sarah lost sight of her.

As Sarah reached the edge of the barnyard, Briny suddenly appeared, running at her shoulder.

"Imogene," Briny screamed.

Sarah could hardly hear her for the howl of the engines. "What?" she screamed back.

"We can't find her! If she's in the barn—" Briny pushed Sarah toward a man who seemed to be controlling the great, yellow monsters.

The man waved at the girls, "Go back, back!"
The girls poured on the speed, running faster toward the tall, slim man in a hard hat. Another man, burly, shirt sleeves rolled up, jumped out of a pickup truck parked next to the farmhouse. He hurried to cut off their path to the foreman.

The ground trembled under the whine of the bulldozers. Acrid exhaust filled Sarah's nose. She thought she saw Lassie through the sagging slats of the old barn, dashing about inside, searching, hunting.

Oh, find her fast!
The burly man caught Sarah's wrist. "What are you girls doing?" he demanded. "We're about to demolish that barn." He deftly caught Briny by her shoulder.

Briny screamed like a wild thing and lunged at him. Surprised, he let Sarah go and grabbed both Briny's arms. She kicked wildly. Freed, Sarah ran for the foreman who was staring at her in some alarm.

He thinks I'm going to attack him, she thought, and could have laughed except it was so horrible.

She pulled up in front of him. He began to back away. Another man appeared from the pickup truck and came running to protect him, she guessed. She blurted out, "A girl's in the barn!"

Both men frowned at her. Sarah panted, her lungs burning more from fear than from running. The foreman leaned closer to her and said, "We checked the barn. No one's in there. What kind of game is this?"

What if Briny was wrong? Imogene could be just hiding somewhere in the bushes. Sarah still had time to dash away and never be seen. Surely the sheriff would be called soon. The workmen must have seen evidence of the kids living in the barn.

Inside the barn, movement flickered, shadows. No, Lassie wasn't wrong. She was inside still searching.

Sarah shook her head and repeated, "My dog is in there now because someone is in there! Hiding! She's scared!"

Briny had been subdued and was limp. The burly man walked over with her, his big hands still on her shoulders. He had a long red scratch on his cheek.

The burly man said, "She says her sister is in there."

"She is!" Both Sarah and Briny hollered.

"Girls, if this is some kind of joke or test to join a club," began the foreman.

"Look!" said Sarah, pointing to the barn door.

Slowly, it opened.

The Children's War

Lassie came out of the door first, nosing it open. Then Imogene slowly followed, one hand buried in the collie's fur.

"Well, I'm a long haired-lover from Liverpool," said the foreman. "Where was she hiding?"

The foreman gave the order for the bulldozers to cut their motors. Sudden silence rushed the barnyard. Sarah relaxed a little. The noise had been like an aching tooth.

The other children, Corey, led by the hand by Gabby, and Gus, appeared out of nearby bushes and out from behind trees. They ran to Briny. Lassie and Imogene picked their way over to Briny, Lassie and the others between the foreman and Imogene.

Briny threw her arms around the little girl. Gabby scolded her, "Imogene, they're going to knock down the barn. Why didn't you come out?"

Imogene said into Briny's neck, but still holding onto Lassie's fur with one hand. "I was scared. But Lassie saved me again."

Again? wondered Sarah, but before she could say anything, the foreman launched into a tirade about stupid kids playing in condemned buildings.

Then to Sarah's shock, Briny—strong, wild Briny—began to shake. Tears dripped off her nose onto her little sister's head. Corey, seeing his sister crying began to bawl and flung himself on the ground.

That did it. Sarah whirled and faced the men. "Can't you see these kids have had enough with losing their home? Just leave them alone. And you should learn to pay better attention before you start knocking down buildings."

Sarah had never talked like that to grown-ups before, and she was shaking almost as badly as Briny. She grabbed Briny and hauled her away from the red-faced foreman.

Since Imogene had a death grip on Briny and Lassie, she followed without a word, and the rest of the kids stumbled after them like a tattered banner. Corey was still steadily howling.

One of the men called, "Hey, you kids were living here?"

They didn't answer. Sarah just hurried everyone away from the farm, straight across the rocky, unkempt fields, the shortest way home she knew. Gabby and Sarah held the barbed wire strands apart and let the kids file through, including Lassie who left a tuft of silky fur on a barb. Imogene snatched the bit of fur and put it in her pocket.

The bulldozers started their engines, growling and

shaking the air behind them. The old barn was soon going to be driven to its knees. Sarah could hardly bear it. The barn had seemed almost alive, like a great, impassive beast.

After the children walked off the farm's boundary lines, they stood on the rise, looking down into what Sarah realized must have once been a handsome sweep of land. The deep green circle of the pond and the willows, the surrounding roll of fields when tended must have been lovely in crops. Even the two-story farmhouse, if freshly painted and windows hung with bright curtains, instead of boarded up, would have been charming. The barn, the curved rafters and beams, like the huge ribs of a sea-going ship, was stately and could have outshone any modern barn easily.

"Look," said Briny. Sarah looked. Then she took her friend's hand.

The bulldozers did their work. The flat side of the barn went down like a draft horse whose legs have been knocked out from under it. The longer front and back sides of the barn poised upright a moment as if resisting the giant machines. Sarah wanted to cheer encouragement, then the whole barn burst apart like a rotten egg. Dust shot up and widened, almost like a thunderhead in the summer.

The sound came delayed.

The huge boom rolled over the fields like an invisible rolling pin. The noise sounded as if monster rams butted heads. Lesser booms and groans flicked in on the heels of the first explosion.

Corey had stopped howling and was in awe of the sound that was louder than any of his shrieks would ever be.

The six children and Lassie watched a long moment. The dust began to telescope back onto itself. The lighter stuff, chaff, very fine dust, drifted on the breeze like heavy pollen.

"Now what?" whispered Briny. Tears shone in her eyes. "We didn't even get our stuff." She was holding long-legged Imogene on her hip. The little girl was wrapped around her sister.

Lassie whined and pushed at Sarah's knees. Home, Lassie seemed to say. Let's go home.

So Sarah gently pulled Briny's hand. "Come on," she said. "We'll go to my house." The children stumbled after, as if shell shocked from a war.

No, Sarah corrected herself. They had been in a war. They'd fought many battles. But now Sarah told herself the war was over. There was no more fight left in any of them. They were going home.

22

Lassie, Everywhere?

Early Friday morning, Lassie pawed at Jimmy's arm. She wanted him to wake up before he had to get ready for school. She pawed again. Wake up! She wanted to bark, but didn't want to wake the others. Jimmy mumbled and turned over. Lassie whined and licked his ear.

"Lassie," he muttered and shoved at her shoulder, but she gripped his wrist in her mouth and tugged at him.

His eyes opened. "Okay, okay, you're worse than any alarm clock. Honestly." He pulled his arm back and sat up.

She wagged her tail as he quietly got dressed. He had to step carefully over the sleeping bodies of Gus and Cal in sleeping bags on his floor.

Jimmy yawned. He hadn't had much sleep. They'd all been up late last night. When he'd finally fallen into bed, he hadn't even looked at the clock, afraid to notice the time. So why was he getting up so early anyway? He still had another hour until he had to get ready for school.

School. Today they would find out who would meet Bl—

131

No, he wouldn't even think about him—it. More important things had happened and been revealed last night. Much more important things.

Wanting to stay in bed, Jimmy sat back down quietly, but Lassie wedged her body between him and the mattress. He gave up. He followed her wagging tail out into the hall. "Is it okay if I go to the bathroom first?"

She sat down and waited patiently until he came back out. Then she seized his jeans leg and pulled him along as if he were a wayward puppy.

"Okay, okay," he laughed, staggering, but following his collie down the stairs and out into the quiet morning.

They ran. The morning air was liquid—smooth, quick, cool. Every breath seemed to go clear down to Jimmy's toes.

Jimmy ran after his gold and white collie. She trotted with determination along the country roads. After five years of owning her, he wondered if a person could really own something as independent as Lassie? He still marveled at her. She was sheer proof that there was a God and that He was good. That much Jimmy knew. God always makes things work out for the good.

They ran and ran, floating east. The sun, blurred by thin clouds, suddenly popped up like a party balloon and threw out streamers of light across the land. Lassie led him straight down the road to the old farm's property where the kids had been living. Living! In an abandoned barn. No wonder Cal had behaved oddly, as Katie put it.

Jimmy slowed. "Why here, Lassie?" She woofed encouragement at him, but he was uneasy coming here. The great mammoth barn was only a fallen pile of ruined timber, yet it was much more. It was like the fall of lives, too.

Last night Dad had said when all the children, including Jimmy and Sarah, were sitting on the couch, chairs, and carpet, eating, that God had a plan for each of them. Dad also said God would honor Cal and Briny's efforts to keep their family together, but that He wouldn't honor the way they had been going about it. Dad promised to check out all possible options, but everyone must agree to do things the right way, the legal way. All the kids had nodded yes.

Then there was his sister, Sarah! Her confession was a shock. She had sat in the old oak rocker, weeping. She had confessed to taking food and money from home, and taking stuff from Wooden's store, and that *she* had been the one to steal the Wacky Rodeo money. The stuff she had done! His sister, his little sister! He could hardly believe his ears.

Then Dad said, "It saddens me to hear this, Sarah, but I'm glad that you told us." At that point, Sarah ran over to Dad and flung her arms around his neck, telling him how sorry she was and that she would never lie and steal again.

At that point, Mom joined the group hug and everyone was crying.

Sarah seemed to grow up right before our eyes, Jimmy

thought. Dad had told her that she'd always carry the scars of stealing and lying, but that God would heal her and make her stronger, if that's what she wanted. It was.

⚓

Lassie sharply barked, snatching him out of the strangeness of last night. She was walking onto some of the shattered, fallen boards on the edge of the main pile.

"Lassie, come," he commanded. The old barn couldn't be any safer fallen. Probably scores of rusted nails, spiders, glass, who knew what else lurked just under the rotten boards.

Lassie steadily ignored his command. Jimmy sighed impatiently and began to follow her onto the pile of the old barn, which was what he knew she wanted. Lassie. She always seemed to get her way somehow.

She sniffed around the lattice work of the boards, searching, whining. What could she be searching for? A board rocked. He gasped, but she jumped lightly out of danger, hardly breaking her sniffing path.

Jimmy, his arms out, balancing, teetered about, knowing what they were doing was stupid, dangerous, and illegal. He could see himself explaining to the authorities, "My dog made me do it." As if he hadn't heard enough blaming and finger pointing from Sarah and the kids.

Lassie stopped over one section and scratched at a pile of boards. It looked like every other pile to him. But she whined and scratched with both front paws.

Jimmy scrambled to her side. He lifted one board, then stepped on another one underneath it. The weak wood fractured and snapped. He lifted the pieces and tossed them away in a clatter. Lassie continued scratching, digging, whining. He moved more debris where she scratched.

Funny, he thought, *under the crisscross of these boards there seems to be a large box, about the size of a pickup truck bed.*

He hauled a couple more boards off. Then he stared, shocked at what sat in the dirt and wood fragments. Lassie gave a triumphant bark and pounced.

Finally! What she had been looking for. She tried to pick it up, but her teeth slipped on the smooth ceramic. Jimmy gently moved her out of his way.

It was his collie bank.

He picked it up. It was in one piece still. That was incredible. He blew off a layer of dust. Lassie sneezed. As if in a dream, Jimmy pulled the plastic plug of the bank. Inside was the wad of checks, all of them and all of the ticket money. Last night Briny had apologized for leaving the money in the barn. Dad had said they'd tell the workmen to keep an eye out for the money, but he doubted it would be found, or if some was found, would the workers really report it? Probably not.

But where the bank had rested, the wad of cash, wrapped tight in a gold-threaded, stretchy sort of hair thing, like Sarah might wear, was safe.

Last night Briny had glanced at Sarah when she said, "I knew the money wasn't from Sarah's savings account, so we didn't spend any of it. We were going to return it some-how." Sarah, of course, had wept and rocked. Only Lassie seemed to know what to do. She had laid her lovely head in Sarah's lap and his sister had been comforted.

Lassie.

Always Lassie. Wherever he turned, Lassie.

Jimmy thought, *Why, that's how God is. He really is everywhere in the world, the universe. And He cares about me. That's got to be one reason God gave us Lassie—to have a wonderful helper when times get tough.*

When the discussion was over last night, Dad had stood. "I think we've all learned the importance of being honest with each other . . . and with God," he had said. "I know from experience that God is more than willing to forgive us and give us a new start. So, I think before we all hit the sack, we should pray together and ask God to forgive us for the things we've done wrong in this situation."

Something really special had happened when they prayed together. Jimmy seemed to sense that the fear each one felt was gone, and they could trust each other again. It gave Jimmy hope that everything would work out—the rodeo, the Freedmans finding a home, his meeting Blair Coughlin, everything.

Lassie was busy digging again.

"More?" asked Jimmy, laughingly. She must be playing now. He had everything back. But he leaned over and helped her pull out from under a chunk of concrete, a plastic bag with toy Indians, horses and cowboys. Satisfied, Lassie held the bag in her mouth and jumped off the pile of what had been the old barn.

Jimmy followed, the bank and the contents safely tucked under his arm.

How had Lassie known? Maybe in some strange way God had told her. Jimmy couldn't say for sure, but he knew that things would never be the same, not for the Freedmans, not for the Harmons, particularly not for Sarah.

Jimmy ran with his collie all the way home to show the others what Lassie had found.

23

You Can Trust a Friend

At the Wacky Rodeo on Saturday, Jimmy stood shoulder to shoulder with Blake on one side and Cal on the other. Lassie was pressed against his legs. They all leaned on the corral fence, watching, laughing, shouting.

The grandstand is full to bursting with people that we sold tickets to, thought Jimmy a little dazed, as if he burst up through the surface of lake water into a strange world. A good world though. Barbecue smoke tantalized the crowd and put people in mind of a good meal. Even Lassie sniffed appreciatively, without taking her gaze from the ruckus in the arena.

Cal started laughing. Jimmy suddenly realized he'd never heard Cal laugh before.

Crazy Katie, much to her family's dismay, had entered the pony bareback bronc riding. Most of the ponies were just local kids' mounts, enticed to buck because of the tight ropes under their tender flanks. Some of the ponies, so well trained to never buck, just stood staring, shocked at the crowd, and drew wild laughter and shouts. The ponies would gawk more, which caused even more laughter.

"Definitely wacky," observed Blake.

In one chute, Katie was swinging onto a chunky brown and white pony. One of the younger classes had been asked to rename the ponies. The loudspeaker announced: "Katie Madison, an eighth grader, is riding Apple Duster Buster! Let her rip, gentlemen."

The gate opened. Apple Duster Buster bolted, Katie clinging to his back, looking like a spider taking a wild ride on a frisbee. Then the pony leaped straight up, sunfishing, all four hooves pursed together as if the pony thought he'd land directly on a pog.

Cal laughed again and shouted, "Hang on, Katie!"

That surprised Jimmy. Cal rooting for Katie?

Hang on Katie did. Actually that was something she was good at, Jimmy realized. And not just ponies, but ideas and projects and people, even if she was rather prickly about it at first.

When Apple Duster Buster visited the ground, it was very momentarily. He sprang back up with a good twist. Katie was on his neck, then she was straddling his hips. Then she was talking to the ground. But not for long. She jumped and bowed. The crowd clapped and shouted.

The loudspeaker said, "Thank you, Katie Madison. She stayed on six seconds. Not bad, not bad." Apple Duster

Buster bucked across the arena until the rodeo cowboys chased him into a pen on the far side.

Katie, dusty as a desert horned toad, ran to the fence where Jimmy and the others were leaning. She dusted off her clothes, spitting mud. Hands helped her, not that she needed it. Jimmy noticed Cal was eager to help. Jimmy wasn't sure he liked that arrangement.

"Want some Coke?" asked Jimmy. She took his cup and drank deep.

"I need a bath," she exclaimed. Jimmy couldn't resist and dumped the ice over her head. She screeched and pounded him and he felt better after that. The rest of the Wacky Rodeo bounced by, silly and fun.

When the last event was over, a drum rolled over the loud speaker.

"Here comes Blair Coughlin!" yelled Blake. Jimmy snatched his pocket camera out of his shirt pocket.

The announcer said, "Here's Iowa's own Blair Coughlin, Colorado Cobras' quarterback, riding Miss Piggy!"

A dappled-gray pony plunged out of the chute. Blair Coughlin could have carried the pony she was so tiny, but she was fiercely strong. The pony galloped around the arena twice, never eaking a sweat. Blair Coughlin waved.

Suddenly Lassie barked cheerfully and dove through the fence into the arena.

"Lassie! Come back here!" hollered Jimmy, but Lassie,

being Lassie, did what she must.

The loudspeaker roared, "Get that dog out of the arena!"

Jimmy, astonished, ducked through the fence after his wayward collie. But he shouldn't have worried about Lassie.

The big collie halted a few feet from the pony. The small equine dropped her nose and the dog and pony sniffed one another. Jimmy ran up, but Blair Coughlin raised a hand and said, "Just a minute." He then sat astride the pony, watching the two animals. Blair Coughlin, the great football player was amused, not mad about the change in plans.

Jimmy, thinking fast, since he was so close to Blair Coughlin, snapped a couple of photos.

Lassie and the gray pony suddenly burst into a chase. First, the pony raced after Lassie, still toting the huge football player. Jimmy, laughing, knew then the pony was Sarah's old pony Gray Feathers and that Lassie had recognized the pony too!

Blair Coughlin sat as best he could on the small back as the pony wove in and out, dancing after the collie. Jimmy snapped picture after picture, laughing so much he was afraid all the frames would be blurry.

After a couple of times around the arena, the pony suddenly slid to a stop, her hindquarters sitting down like a reining horse, and Blair Coughlin tipped right off. Lassie gave a surprised yip.

The football player turned a somersault and landed on his rear in the dust. Lassie ran up to him and Blair Coughlin petted her.

Jimmy reached him just before the rodeo clowns came in and Blair Coughlin winked and said, "Don't tell anybody this wasn't part of the program, okay?"

Jimmy agreed, laughing, and held out his hand to help his hero up as Lassie and the pony took off for one more turn around the arena.

❧

Behind the grandstand Blair Coughlin was signing autographs and photos. The line was huge. For a special prize, any of the eighth-grade class could have a photo taken of himself with Blair Coughlin.

"Did you get a picture?" Katie asked Jimmy.

He shook his head. "I gave Cal my turn."

She stared at him. "What do you mean?"

Jimmy's face grew hot. "When it was my turn in line, I asked Blair Coughlin if he would tell Cal about KidsTown during the time I would have had my picture taken with him."

Katie hung on the railing. "But you wanted to talk to him so much and get his photo."

"I know," said Jimmy. "But it's okay." It hurt. He'd been working hard so he could meet his hero, but in a funny way, Lassie had introduced him. He figured some of his photos would come out okay. Plus it really was more important that Cal talk with Blair. And Blair had actually stopped the autograph signing and picture taking for about fifteen minutes, and had taken Cal aside and talked with him.

Jimmy had seen the glow on Cal's face and was really glad he'd said something, but he knew Cal wouldn't have done it for himself.

"So are you ready to go?" Katie asked.

Just then Cal and Lassie, who had stayed with Cal, ran up to Jimmy and Katie.

"He's so great," exclaimed Cal. "He told me a little about living at KidsTown. Then he gave me his phone number and told me to call him collect next week to talk some more."

"You're kidding," said Jimmy, stunned. Then he said, "He's a real hero."

Cal laughed. "That's funny, because he said that about you and about me!"

"Us!"

"He said we're all real-life heroes," explained Cal, "because of all we've been through and done to help each other." Cal patted Lassie, then said slyly, "I hope you didn't mind, but I got this sudden idea." Cal leaned over and unbuckled Lassie's collar. "Look," he said and thrust the collar at Jimmy.

Written in bold black letters around Lassie's collar read: Blair Coughlin, 42, Colorado Cobras.

"All right," breathed Jimmy. "Thanks, Cal."

"I felt bad you didn't get to talk with him like you wanted," said Cal. They began to walk away from the arena.

"I'm still thirsty," said Katie. "Let's get something to drink."

They stood at the concession stand where Sarah was working so she could pay back what she'd taken from Mom and Dad and from Wooden's Drug Store. Briny was also working at another concession stand.

Jimmy, Katie, Cal, and Lassie stood in Sarah's line. They ordered and got their drinks. Sarah served Jimmy last.

When she handed him his change, he pocketed the money instantly.

"Better count it," she warned him, joking a little, but yet her voice wobbled.

Jimmy said, firmly, "I don't need to, Sarah, I trust you."

She smiled.

The funny thing was he did trust her.

Families were like that, he guessed as he walked off with his friends. Friends were like that too. You could trust them without looking.